Quincannon

Chapter 1

The cable car clattered downhill on Sutter Street, toward where the lamps lining Market shone a blurred yellow through the rain-damp night. One of the lighted buildings below was the Reception Saloon; but Quincannon, riding outside in spite of the weather, paid no attention to its beckoning glow. Once he would have marked the nearness of the Reception with keen anticipation, but for almost a year now he had done his public drinking in Hoolihan's Irish Pub, south of Market, where the liquor was cheaper and the patrons more interested in their drinks than in their drinking companions.

When the car slowed for its Market Street terminus, Quincannon dropped off. It was a chill night, with a sharp wind that slashed in from the Bay, and he drew up the collar of his greatcoat. But he scarcely felt the cold. The whiskey he had taken in his rooms on Leavenworth still warmed him like a banked fire.

He walked swiftly through the light rain, down Market in the direction of the Ferry Building — a big man, dark-haired under his derby hat, with a heavy gray-shot beard and an unsmiling countenance that gave him, falsely, the look of a freebooter. It was a weeknight, just before nine o'clock, and traffic was sparse: a few pedestrians hurrying from one saloon to another, a pair of lighted trolleys passing nearby, a lone hack looking for a fare, two or three carriages with their side-curtains drawn. From somewhere on the Bay, a foghorn gave its lonesome cry. A poor night for ships, a worse one for men like himself, out on business and mostly sober.

At Second Street he turned right and soon entered Hoolihan's. It was crowded, as always in the evenings, its clientele composed for the most part of tradesmen, small merchants, office workers, and a somewhat rougher element up from the waterfront. No city leaders came here on their nightly rounds, as they did to the Reception, the Palace Hotel bar, Pop Sullivan's Hoffman Café, and the other first-class saloons along the Cocktail Route; no judges, politicians, bankers, and gay young blades in their striped trousers, fine cravats, and brocaded waistcoats. Hoolihan's had no crystal candelabra, fancy mirrors, expensive oil paintings, white-coated barmen, or elaborate free lunch. It was dark and bare by comparison, with sawdust thick-scattered on the floor and the only glitter and sparkle coming from the shine of its gaslights on the ranks of bottles and glasses along the backbar. And its free lunch consisted of staple fare: corned beef, strong cheese, rye bread, pots of mustard, and tubs of briny pickles.

Quincannon liked it better than any of the first-class saloons, and not only because it suited his need for privacy. It was an honest place, made for honest men and honest drinking. Far fewer lies were told in Hoolihan's than in the rarified atmosphere of the Reception, he suspected, and far fewer dark deeds were hatched.

He made his way through the throng to the far corner of the bar, his customary place. He had an hour before he was due to meet Bonniwell, which allowed the better part of forty-five minutes to fortify himself. The edge he had maintained from his rooms was beginning to fade and the Virginia City images were gathering again: he could see Katherine Bennett's face at the periphery of his mind, hear her screams; and the pain this brought him, as always, was too much to endure sober.

He ordered a double shot, drank it off, and ordered a second with a beer chaser. When the second whiskey was gone the images and the ghostly cries were at bay again. He took his pipe and plug of tobacco from the pocket of his frock coat, busied his hands preparing a smoke.

Time passed. Quincannon thought about helping himself to the corned beef and rye bread, but even though he hadn't eaten since noon, he had no appetite. He called to the barman for a third whiskey; but when it came he let it sit untouched, sipping his beer instead. He would take it just before he went out into the night again — that would be soon enough. His thoughts would have to be clear when he talked to Bonniwell.

Thinking of the little wharf rat and police informant guided his hand to his trouser pocket, to the counterfeit half eagle he carried there. Absently, he ran his thumb over its edge. Fair craftsmanship. Much better had gone into the counterfeit ten-dollar note tucked into a corner of his billfold; the engraver who had designed the plates was a man of rare talent. The most accomplished koniakers he had come up against in ten years, this bunch. And the cleverest by far. If Bonniwell —

"Quincannon, isn't it?" a voice said at his elbow. "John Quincannon?"

He turned to face a tubby man wearing muttonchop whiskers and a Prince Albert, with an ivory-headed cane looped over his arm. The round, red face was somewhat familiar, but he couldn't quite place a name to it. He had no desire for casual conversation on this night — on any night in the past year — and rudeness was the best way to avoid it. He turned back to his drinks without making a reply.

But the tubby man wedged in alongside him and hooked a polished vici kid shoe over the brass rail. "Perhaps you don't recall me, sir. The name is Muldauer, William Muldauer. Reporter for the San Francisco *News*. I interviewed you once — let me see, four years ago, I think it was. Yes. The Barlow case. Altered wildcat banknotes, if you'll remember."

Quincannon remembered. He also remembered Muldauer, now, along with the fact that he hadn't cared for the man at the time of the interview. He remained silent, reaching for his beer.

Muldauer would not be put off. "You *are*

still with the Secret Service, Mr. Quin-cannon? A man of your abilities . . . yes, of course you are. Are you at liberty to discuss your current work, by any chance?"

Quincannon drank from his stein, wiped foam off his mustache. The Seth Thomas on the wall above the backbar gave the time as twenty-five of ten. He would have to leave soon if he expected to reach Bonniwell's rooming house by ten o'clock.

"I should be delighted to have another interview," Muldauer said. He leaned closer and breathed the odor of shandygaff into Quincannon's face. If there was one drink Quincannon hated it was shandygaff; diluting good beer with ginger ale was an abomination. "I can guarantee that my editor will pay ten dollars for the privilege."

Damn your editor, Quincannon thought, and almost gave voice to the words. Instead he said, "I'm not interested, Mr. Muldauer. I can't and won't speak about my present activities. Now if you don't mind —"

"Secret work, eh?" Muldauer said. "It wouldn't have anything to do with the coney greenbacks that have flooded the coast the past few months, would it?"

"No, it wouldn't."

"Ah! Of course not." Muldauer gave him

12

a conspiratorial wink, and Quincannon realized that the man was more than a little drunk. Too drunk to be insulted; too drunk to be gotten rid of in an ordinary fashion. "Who's behind the game, sir? Any speculations? Some say it's a gang in Seattle, led by an old queersman name Schindler. What would *you* say, Mr. Quincannon? Off the record, naturally. A passing remark."

Quincannon lifted the shot glass, drained the whiskey at a swallow, and nudged the tubby reporter away from him. "Good night, Mr. Muldauer," he said, and moved off across the crowded room without looking back.

But when he reached the door he felt a tug at his coat sleeve and saw that Muldauer had followed him. He shrugged off the hand, stepped out into the misty darkness. Muldauer, still persistent, came after him.

"If you won't discuss your current work, Mr. Quincannon, perhaps a past case? Eh? Our readers are always interested in good detective work, and you've a reputation for it. The Stanley case in Virginia City comes to mind. Details are meager; we should all like to know more."

Quincannon stood rigid, but he was trembling inside. "No," he said.

13

"But why not? Is it because of the woman who was killed? What was her name? Katherine —"

He moved without thinking about it; he caught hold of the lapels of Muldauer's Prince Albert and threw him up against the saloon wall, hard enough to send the fat man's derby hat flying. Breath came out of Muldauer's mouth in a surprised, frightened grunt. He slapped at Quincannon's hands with fluttery gestures, like a woman.

"Here, here, what's this? You can't —"

"Shut up," Quincannon said. "And leave me be from now on, Muldauer. Do your drinking somewhere else. If you bother me again I'll give you worse than this."

He let go of the newspaperman and stepped back. Muldauer brushed and tugged at his Prince Albert; moved to pick up his derby hat from the puddled cobbles. In the out-spill of lamplight from Hoolihan's front window, his round face was pinched and outraged.

"You can't manhandle me for no reason!" he shouted. "I won't stand for it!" He jammed the derby down on his head and pointed a shaking finger at Quincannon. "I'll report this incident to your superior! By God, I'll write a story about it! See if I won't, you . . . you damned flycop!"

14

Quincannon put his back to the man and walked away through the rain.

At Market Street he turned east again, toward the Ferry Building. The whiskey in him no longer dulled his thoughts or kept the pain at bay; the encounter with Muldauer had seen to that. Damn the fat toad. Another enemy made — and hardly the first over the past twelve months. Likely Muldauer would make good his threats to talk to Boggs, to write an exaggerated account of the incident for the *News*. Well, so be it. Others had reported him to Boggs, if not to the public at large, and nothing had come of it. Warnings, yes. Admonishments to mind his temper, curtail his drinking. But Boggs would never recommend dismissal from the Service, not without major provocation. A damned flycop John Quincannon was, in more ways than one, but also a damned *good* flycop. As good as his father had been.

Not that it mattered so much if he was given the sack — not any more. Quincannon's work was all he had left of his life, and he pursued it doggedly; but if it were taken away from him he would feel little regret. A temporary inconvenience was all it would be, until he could find some other means of earning the price of his lodging and his liquor.

He was nearing the Embarcadero now. Ahead, the massive bulk of the Ferry Building appeared through the thin drizzle; and on either side of it, the pier sheds and the masts and steam funnels of anchored ships, like a burned-out forest silhouetted against the black sky. Quincannon turned right again on Spear Street, went along its deserted length to Folsom. The buildings here, close to the docks, were a mixture of warehouses, stores operated by ships' chandlers and outfitters, and seamen's rooming houses. The rooming house in which Bonniwell lived lay just ahead, close to Harrison Street and the pier at its foot.

As he walked, Quincannon kept his eye sharp for footpads. Muggings were not so common here as in the Barbary Coast, that seat of sin north of Market, but the waterfront was still a rough area at night; a man alone, particularly a man dressed in other than seaman's garb, was fair prey — and no matter that he might be armed, as Quincannon was. But he saw no one. And heard nothing except for the foghorns on the Bay, the distant muffled throb of a piano from one of the saloons on the Embarcadero.

Bonniwell's rooming house took shape in

the darkness — a three-story firetrap made of warping wood, never painted and badly in need of carpentry work. Smears of lamplight showed at the front entrance, in three windows in the near wall. A fenced pipeyard occupied the lot on the near side, with an alleyway separating it from the rooming house; the building on the far side was a rope-and-twine chandler's.

Movement at one of the lighted windows caught Quincannon's attention, gave him pause. The window was on the third floor, and the movement appeared to be a struggle between two men . . . no, a heavy-set man half-carrying, half-dragging the limp form of a smaller man. The sash had been thrown up. Quincannon realized the heavy-set man was bent on pushing the other one out through the opening.

Quincannon broke into a run; he knew without counting windows that the room was Bonniwell's. But he made no move to draw the Remington double-action Navy revolver from its holster under his coat. He had not drawn it against a man since that day in Virginia City and would not again, even to save his life, unless he were in close quarters with no one else close by — and even then he could not be sure he would be able to fire it at another human being.

Instead, now, he shouted as he ran; shouted a second time. The heavy-set man's head jerked up at the cries, and Quincannon had a clear impression of a square-slabbed face topped by fiery red hair. He yelled a third time, but neither his shouts nor his presence checked the red-head's actions.

The small man came toppling out of the window headfirst, struck the side of the building, and fell in a loose sprawl. Quincannon, at the alley mouth now, turning into it, saw the body hit the muddy ground, heard the dull breaking sound it made. He looked up again. The red-haired man was gone from the window.

Quincannon ran past where the body lay, to the rear of the alley. The redhead would not go down and out the front way, where he would properly expect to meet the person who had just witnessed his crime. He would come down the back stairs instead. There was no doubt of that in Quincannon's mind; he knew desperate men, knew how they thought. He had been a desperate man himself more than once.

A six-foot board fence turned the alley into a dead-end. Without slowing he caught hold of the top boards and hoisted himself up and over. The rear door of the rooming house banged open just as he dropped down on the far side; the red-haired man emerged at a run, brandishing a pistol. The ground on this side of the fence was a quagmire; Quincannon's feet slid out from under him and he went down hard in the mud. The fall saved his life, for the redhead fired twice and both bullets smacked into the boards directly behind him.

The red-haired man kept on running across the yard, into the shadow of a pepper tree. Quincannon, struggling to get his feet under him, heard thumping noises at the far boundary fence as the fugitive clambered over it. By the time he reached the fence himself, the man had vanished into the misty darkness.

Quincannon slapped mud off his hands and clothing, then returned to the alley fence. Men clogged the rooming house's rear doorway now, peering out, talking in excited voices; he paid no attention to them. He climbed the fence again, went to where the body lay, and knelt beside it.

The dead face that stared up at him, as he had known it would be, was Bonniwell's.

Other men came cautiously into the alley, one of them carrying a lighted lantern. Quincannon identified himself, showed his Service badge, and then appropriated the lantern and used its light to examine Bonniwell. The little informant's skull had been shattered, perhaps in the fall and perhaps in his room by some sort of blunt instrument. There was nothing in his pockets that indicated what he might have found out about the koniakers — the knowledge that had doubtless led to his murder. But there *was* something in his clenched right hand, something he had managed to conceal there before being struck down, something the red-haired man had overlooked.

Quincannon pried it loose with some difficulty. It was a wadded piece of butcher's paper. Shielding it from the rain with his coat, he uncrumpled the paper and read what was written on it.

Whistling Dixon
Silver City, Idaho

20

Chapter 2

Early the next morning, Quincannon was the first to arrive at the Secret Service field office in the U.S. Mint at Fifth and Mission streets — one of the rare occasions that anyone had ever come in ahead of Boggs. The small, cramped room smelled of steam heat and Boggs' Havana cigars; Quincannon opened one of the windows overlooking Mission Street to let in cold, moist air. He had taken two drinks before leaving his rooms, as was his custom every day, and he took another now from his pocket flask — a small one, to keep his thoughts sharp at the center and dull at the edges. Then he sat down at his cluttered desk.

There were three desks in the office, the largest belonging to Boggs; the third was assigned to young Samuel Greenspan, who was now somewhere in the Pacific Northwest following a different lead on the counterfeiting case. Boggs, Greenspan, and

Quincannon composed the main staff of the San Francisco office. Boggs, in fact, had been one of the original thirty operatives brought together to form the Service in 1865, more than twenty-five years ago, and had been handpicked to open this office, one of eleven scattered throughout the country. Before that, he had been a private detective in Washington, D.C., specializing in counterfeiting cases, and a personal friend of both Quincannon's father and William P. Wood, the first Chief of the Service. Rumor had it that Boggs had also helped to draw up the original list of six general orders that he kept framed on the wall above his desk. He had quoted those articles for so long and so often, verbatim, that Quincannon had them memorized, too.

1. Each man must recognize that his service belongs to the government through 24 hours of every day.
2. All must agree to assignment to the locations chosen by the Chief, and respond to whatever mobility of movement the work might require.
3. All must exercise such careful saving of money spent for travel, subsistence, and payments for information as can be self-evidently justified.

4. Continuing employment in the Service will depend upon demonstrated fitness, ability as investigators, and honesty and fidelity in all transactions.
5. The title of regular employees will be Operative, Secret Service. Temporary employees will be Assistant Operatives or Informants.
6. All employment will be at a daily pay rate; accounts submitted monthly. Each operative will be expected to keep on hand enough personal reserve funds to carry on Service business between paydays.

Article 3 had been a constant bone of contention during the ten years Quincannon had worked in the San Francisco office. What he considered justified expenditures seldom coincided with Boggs' opinion; their arguments had been mostly amiable, like an ongoing chess match each of them looked forward to — Quincannon for the challenge of finding a winning gambit, Boggs because he almost always won. That had been the case, at least, until the incident in Nevada the previous year. Now it was Article 4 that Boggs most often quoted — the continuing fitness and ability of Quincannon as an investigator. But he raised the issue gently, knowing as he did the full story of Katherine Bennett's death and understanding what it had done to Quincannon. Boggs was not a man who generally yielded to personal feelings — the Service came first and foremost in his life — but he made allowances in this instance, out of a combination of loyalty, friendship, and pity. Quincannon did not really care one way or the other. He walled out Boggs and Boggs' attitude as he walled out everything and everyone else: using pain for bricks and alcohol for mortar.

In the bottom drawer of his desk were a number of maps of the Western states and territories. He found the one for Idaho and spread it open. Silver City was in the southwestern corner of the state, in the Owyhee Mountains where the barren, unsettled corners of Oregon and Idaho met the equally barren Nevada desert — a silver-mining town that had been the center of a boom in the 1870s and was still a major producer of that precious metal. The closest rail service was at Nampa, just north of Boise, forty miles away; from there an overland trip via stage or horseback was required. Police jurisdiction in the area, Quincannon thought, would be thin and divided, thereby making it a favorite haunt of outlaws from four different states.

He took down the government survey pamphlet on Idaho and read what it contained about Silver City and the Owyhee region. Then, from his wallet, he removed the slip of paper he had found last night in Bonniwell's hand and studied that again. He was still studying it when Boggs came in.

Boggs was in his mid-fifties, a round, graying man with a bulbous nose; one of his friends had once likened him to a keg of whiskey with the nose as its bung. He favored butternut suits, fashionable square-crown hats, and gold-headed walking sticks in a variety of designs. The stick he carried this morning bore the head of a lion.

His surprise at seeing Quincannon at his desk so early was evident. He said, "Well, this establishes a happy precedent," and immediately went to the open window and banged it shut. Then he lit one of his Havana panatellas. He liked the office warm, even stuffy, and redolent of cigar smoke.

Quincannon said, "Bonniwell was murdered last night. Bludgeoned to death in his rooming house and the body dropped into the alley below to make it seem an accident."

Boggs gave him a narrow, glowering look. "How do you know it was murder?"

"I saw the man responsible. He pushed the body through the window just as I was approaching."

"And?"

"He escaped. I almost caught him."

"Almost," Boggs said heavily. "Were you drunk?"

"No. The rain and the muddy ground were to blame, not liquor."

"Did you have a good look at him?"

"Red-thatched, big, face mindful of a slab of marble. I've never seen him before. But I'll know him if I see him again."

"Was there anything in Bonniwell's room?"

"Nothing. The redhead saw to that. But I did find something in Bonniwell's hand."

"And that was?"

Quincannon stood and brought the piece of butcher's paper to Boggs, who squinted at it through the smoke from his cigar.

"Whistling Dixon," Boggs said. "Someone's name?"

"No doubt. It means nothing to me."

"Nor to me."

26

Boggs went to his desk, sat down, and lifted out the file on the present case from the bottom drawer. Quincannon stood watching him shuffle through reports from a variety of sources both here in the West and in Washington; samples of the silver eagles and half eagles that had first begun to appear in Oregon, Washington State, and northern California close to a year ago; samples of the ten- and twenty-dollar notes that were now flooding the entire coast, as well as Nevada, Idaho, Montana, and Utah, and had been for better than three months; lists of known counterfeiters, coney brokers, and boodle carriers. But it was a slim file, for all of that. Scattered bits of positive information, a welter of speculation and possibilities.

Neither the coins nor the greenbacks bore the style of any known counterfeiter. The ink and the silk-fiber paper that were being used to make the notes were of good quality and therefore would not have come cheap, but their source or sources remained a mystery. None of the counterfeit seemed to have been transported or distributed in a traceable fashion, through known carriers or brokers. The only definite link between the coins and greenbacks had come from a field operative in Seattle, who had managed to trace a man who had shoved $10,000 worth of queer on a local brokerage house. When the operative and the local authorities broke into the man's rented flat they found a small cache of both eagles and bills. The man himself had not turned up until two days later — floating in Puget Sound with his face shot away. All efforts to identify him had failed. Samuel Greenspan was still working on that angle, still chasing down what his latest telegram referred to as "dead-end leads" in the Seattle area.

Boggs sat back after a time and licked his cigar from one side of his mouth to the other. "Not a whisper of Silver City anywhere in here," he said, tapping the file. "Did Bonniwell mention the place to you in any context?"

"No," Quincannon said. "He had met someone who might be a boodle carrier for the gang and hoped to have more information for me last night — that was all."

"This carrier's name was Smith, he said?"

"Yes. A phony moniker, of course."

"Bonniwell didn't know where Smith was living?"

"Evidently not. He had met the man in a saloon."

"No lead there, then. Not that we'll need to worry about that, if Whistling Dixon and Silver City prove meaningful." Boggs frowned abruptly. "John, could that piece of paper have been planted in Bonniwell's hand? To put us off on a false scent?"

"There's a chance of it, yes," Quincannon said. "But the handwriting is Bonniwell's — I've seen it before — and the paper was clenched so tight in his fingers that I had difficulty prying it loose. If the redhead put it there the grip would not have been half so tight."

Boggs nodded and sat silent for a time, worrying his cigar. Then he said musingly, "Silver City, eh? Not such a bad place for koniakers to set up shop. Isolated, and not much in the way of law enforcement. Plenty of silver for the coney coins, too."

"It also fits geographically," Quincannon said. "Not far from there to Portland, Seattle, or San Francisco. They could make shipment by freight wagon, even by train from Boise under false bills of lading."

"A risky business, though. Freighting paper and ink, machinery, other supplies into those mountains, then freighting out the queer. Any number of things could go wrong."

"But nothing has. They're a cocky

bunch, and well-organized — that's plain. And in the normal course of events, who would suspect a coney operation in such a place?"

"Just as you say," Boggs agreed.

Quincannon said, "I can be on a train leaving Oakland this afternoon, Mr. Boggs. And in Silver City in two days."

"You can and you will. Use an assumed name and occupation; you'll need to take every precaution."

"I had already planned on that."

Boggs allowed a few seconds to pass and then said, "John . . . you know how important this case is. If we don't put these queersmen out of business, and damned soon, they have the potential to undermine the West's economic system. The entire *country's* economic system, if they should step up production and distribution to the East."

Quincannon said nothing. He knew what was coming.

"I would go to Silver City myself if I could, but I'm needed here. And Greenspan hasn't enough experience. You're the only man I can send; next to me, you're the best operative in this part of the country." There was no false modesty in Boggs; he knew his talents and was not chary about expressing them to others. "Or you were once," he went on pointedly. "If this were twelve months ago I would have no qualms. None at all. But now . . ."

"Do you expect me to burrow up in Silver City with a keg of whiskey?" Quincannon asked.

"Of course not. But a steady consumption of liquor distorts a man's judgment, slows his reflexes, makes him prone to mistakes."

"I won't make any mistakes."

"You might if you continue to drink as you have this past year."

"What is it you want, Mr. Boggs? My promise not to use whiskey while I'm in Silver City?"

"Yes."

"Then you have it."

Boggs looked surprised. "On your word of honor as a gentleman and an employee of the Service?"

"On my word of honor."

This seemed to relieve Boggs and thus put a quick end to what might otherwise have been a lengthy lecture. They spent the next few minutes settling on Quincannon's assumed name and occupation — Andrew Lyons, patent medicine drummer, an alias and a cover he had used before —

and on other matters relative to his mission. Then Quincannon left to return to his rooms, pack a bag, wait for a messenger to deliver a sample case of patent medicine, and then to proceed by ferry to the Oakland railroad depot.

But he made one stop on his way home, at a Market Street saloon not far from the Mint, where he took two whiskeys. He would have another drink in his rooms, and one on the ferry, and one at the depot, and several on the train, and more in Boise and Nampa — and as much as he needed in Silver City. He could not stop drinking there, any more than he could stop here; he had no desire to quit, because sobriety meant confronting the shrieking ghost of Katherine Bennett and that in turn meant madness. He had willfully lied to Boggs and he felt no remorse for having done so. "On my word of honor," he had said. But there was no honor left to him; he had lost it forever. So what did it matter if he added "liar" to what he already was?

And what he was, plain and simple, was a murderer. The murderer of Katherine Bennett, a twenty-year-old woman innocent of any crime and eight months pregnant, who had died screaming with his bullet in her stomach.

Chapter 3

Idaho had changed considerably since the last time Quincannon had been there, nine years ago on a case involving broken-bank bills — notes drawn on a bank that had suspended operation. Back then, in 1884, Boise had been a quiet little town just beginning to grow. Rail service had just been extended all the way across southern Idaho, ending the area's isolation: prior to that year, more than two hundred miles in any direction separated Boise from the nearest railhead or steamboat. The railroads had opened up the area to settlement, with the result that the rich soil of the Snake River Valley now burgeoned with farms and Boise itself had grown into a city of more than four thousand.

Rail tracks had recently been laid into the town proper, and it was at a brand-new depot that the Central Pacific train from Portland delivered Quincannon on Sunday afternoon, two days after his departure from San Francisco. He made arrangements there for passage to Nampa on the Idaho Central, found he had a wait of two hours before the next train, and used that time to find a saloon and slake his thirst with two large whiskeys and a glass of beer. He also bought a bottle of whiskey to take with him; the two he had brought from California were empty, and his pocket flask was nearly so.

It was dusk when he arrived in Nampa, a hamlet still in its infancy that had sprung up along the Oregon Short Line railroad connecting Wyoming with Bear River and the Snake River Valley. The weather was some warmer here than in Boise — a welcome change from the dreary early-fall rains that drenched northern California. He sought out the stage depot, but it was closed for the day. A schedule in its front window told him that the coach to Silver City departed at nine in the morning.

There was a hotel in Nampa, if it could be dignified by that term; but Quincannon cared nothing for comfort any more. He took a room for the night, drew the shade, had his customary nightcap, and took himself to bed.

But sleep eluded him, as it sometimes

did when he was traveling. After a time, restless, he lighted the lamp and tried to read the volume of poems by Emily Dickinson from his warbag. He had three-score volumes of poetry in his rooms in San Francisco, given to him by his mother, and he habitually took one with him on his trips. He had seldom opened any during the past year, but still he packed one. Old habits, good habits, died hard.

I took my power in my hand
And went against the world;
'Twas not so much as David had,
But I was twice as bold.

I aimed my pebble, but myself
Was all the one that fell.
Was it Goliath was too large,
Or only I too small?

He put the book aside, reached for the bottle to pour himself another drink. Poetry. Once he had loved it, just as his mother had; now there was too much meaning in most of it, too many reminders of what he had done and what he was.

He was glad his mother had not lived to hear about Katherine Bennett. She had died much too young, of a disease that had left her withered and riddled with pain. Not that pain had been a stranger to her. A gentlewoman, Margaret Cullen Quincannon, a product of the Virginia aristocracy who had fought on the wrong side during the Civil War and had never been able to reconcile their losses. Life had been good to her before the hostilities; she had married a handsome Scot from Washington, moved to the capital, had a son, sipped cordials and broken bread with heads of state. But then the war had come, and while her loyalties were with the South, her staunchly pro-Union husband had forced her to stay in Washington, in the midst of the Northern effort to crush the Confederacy. One of her brothers had been killed at Bull Run; her father had died of apoplexy shortly before Lee's surrender at Appomattox Court House. The laughter and joy of her youth turned to sorrow and melancholy, to the pain that had stayed with her, growing, for the rest of her days.

She had died bewildered, had Margaret Cullen Quincannon. With nothing left to her but faded memories of a time of gentility that had become a time of blood — and her pride in her only son's success as a detective, first with his father's Washington agency, where he had begun work as a runner and office boy at the age of seventeen, and then with the Secret Service. If she had known about Katherine Bennett, it would have shaken that pride and caused her even more pain.

Thomas L. Quincannon would not have understood either, if *he* were still alive; if an assassin's bullet had not cut him down on the Baltimore docks eleven months after the death of his wife. A stone-hard man, his father; stubborn, unyielding. A man of principle. The rival of Pinkerton, the *better* of Pinkerton to hear him tell it. And a damned old fool who had believed himself invincible, who should not have been on the Baltimore docks the night he was shot, who should have been home in bed like other stout and gout-ridden men his age.

"You shot a pregnant woman by accident," he would have said to his son, "in the performance of your sworn duty to the government of your country. It was unavoidable. Unfortunate, of course, but nonetheless an accident. Put it behind you, John. Forget it. There is no purpose in remorse. What is done is done and cannot be undone." No, Thomas Quincannon would not have understood at all.

Quincannon had taken his father's profession, had worked with his father, had inherited his father's ability for detective work. But inside, at the core of him, he was his mother's son.

He awoke at dawn with a throbbing head and a queasy stomach: it had taken two more drinks to bring him the temporary oblivion of sleep. He took another now, to still the inner trembling, and then doused his head with water from the bureau pitcher, dressed, packed his warbag. Downstairs in the dining room, he forced himself to eat a small breakfast and to wash the food down with two cups of coffee. The second cup he laced with whiskey from his flask, and when he was done with it he felt well enough for travel.

At the stage depot he bought passage for Silver City and sat down to wait for the coach to arrive. He did nothing while he waited; simply sat with his mind blank. Two men came in after a while, both well-dressed, and he looked at them more closely when he heard them purchase tickets for Silver City. One was tall, spare, middle-aged, with a distinguished mane of hemp-colored hair; the other was roly-poly, apple-cheeked, balding, and fortyish. Judging from snippets of their conversation,

Quincannon concluded the two men knew each other but were not traveling together.

The men sat on the far side of the waiting room and continued their conversation desultorily, as if they really had little to say to each other. Quincannon shut his eyes for a time. He opened them when he again heard the sound of the door, saw a woman come in — and then came to his feet with such violence that he kicked over his chair, sent it clattering across the floor.

He was looking at a ghost — the ghost of Katherine Bennett.

At the sudden noise the woman swung around to face him. He saw then that the resemblance was superficial, that it was only in profile that she might have been Katherine Bennett's twin: the same tall, slender form, the same facial bone structure, the same black hair worn long about her shoulders. But the moment had left him badly shaken; his hands twitched, his body was filmed in sweat.

The woman was staring at him, as were the two men across the room. She said, with puzzlement but without anxiety, "Is something wrong?"

"No," he said, "no, it —" The words clogged in his throat. He shook his head, moved away to the door, outside into the warming air.

There was no one near the stable at the rear. He leaned against the depot wall, drank quickly from his flask. The whiskey steadied him, steadied his thoughts. Was the woman another passenger for Silver City? He was not sure how he would bear up under a long ride with her, in the close confines of a Concord coach.

But he had no choice in the matter: when the stage clattered in a few minutes later, the woman was the first to board. She gave him a curious look as the driver helped her in; so did the roly-poly man and the one with the hemp-colored hair. Quincannon let the three of them get settled, waiting until all the luggage had been stowed in the boot and the driver was ready to depart before he steeled himself and swung inside.

The woman was sitting on the seat that faced forward, the tall man beside her. Quincannon occupied the space next to the fat man and opposite the woman, who gave him another curious glance. The fat man must have smelled the sharp odor of whiskey on his breath; he muttered something about strong drink so early in the day. Quincannon paid no attention to him.

In spite of himself he could not take his eyes from the woman.

She was perhaps thirty, attractive in a quiet, mature way. She wore a knitted shoulder cape over a gray traveling dress, and a rather fancy summer leghorn hat. There was strength in the shape of her face and mouth, intelligence in eyes the dark color of the sea at dusk. He found himself both fascinated and repelled.

The four of them sat in silence as the driver climbed onto the box and kicked off the brake and the stage jerked into motion. There was some polite talk after that, among the woman and the two men; they were all acquainted, though evidently not too well. None of them spoke to Quincannon until the stage rumbled aboard the ferry across the Snake River. Then the tall man stepped out to smoke a pipe at the railing, and a few moments later the fat one moved to join him. Quincannon shifted on the leather seat and tried in vain not to look at the woman.

She said abruptly, "Why do you keep staring at me?" But there was still no anxiety in her voice, nor any anger; only curiosity.

"I apologize for that," he said. "My manners are generally much better."

"Do I remind you of someone?"

". . . Yes."

"A loved one?"

"No, not that."

"Someone you knew well, then."

"Someone I never knew at all."

"I'm afraid I don't understand. . . ."

"A private matter," Quincannon said shortly.

"And you would rather not discuss it."

"No. Do you live in Silver City, miss?"

"I do now. I've a milliner's shop there."

"Would you know a man named Whistling Dixon?"

"That's an odd name," she said. "No, I've never heard it before. Is he a friend of yours?"

"Yes."

"And is he what brings you to Silver City?"

"No, business does."

"What is your business, if you don't mind my asking?"

"Salts."

"Salts? Do you mean patent medicines?"

"Dr. Wallmann's Nerve and Brain Salts. The finest blood purifier on the market today, guaranteed to —"

She held up her hand. "Please," she said, smiling slightly, "I'm not a prospective customer, Mr. — ?"

"Lyons, Andrew Lyons."

"I'm Sabina Carpenter. Now that we're acquainted, I'll feel better about being stared at. Assuming you intend to continue."

He didn't smile. "I will try to control myself."

"It gave you quite a start when you first saw me, didn't it?"

"Yes. Quite a start."

Silence for a few moments. Then she said, "May I ask an impertinent question, Mr. Lyons?"

"As you like."

"Do you always drink whiskey so early in the day?"

Quincannon said seriously, "Yes, I do. I'm a drunkard."

"I see," she said, as if he had just told her he was a Presbyterian. "But a harmless one, I trust."

Harmless, he thought. He said nothing.

"Are you proud of your drunkenness, Mr. Lyons, that you speak of it so frankly?"

"Hardly that. But I see no point in telling a lie when the truth will suffice."

"An honest man. How refreshing."

"Don't you know many honest men, Miss Carpenter?"

"Not as many as I would like to."

"The two gentlemen riding with us — are they honest men?"

"I don't know either of them well enough to judge," she said. "At least they are both influential men."

"Oh? In Silver City?"

"Yes. The fat one is Oliver Truax, owner of the Paymaster mine. The Paymaster is one of the largest and richest on War Eagle Mountain."

"You say that as if you have a proprietary interest in it."

"I do, as a matter of fact. I recently bought several shares of stock in the Paymaster Mining Company. You wouldn't happen to be interested in that sort of investment yourself, would you, Mr. Lyons?"

"Not I. I haven't the money for it."

Outside, one of the ferrymen shouted to someone on shore; through the door window Quincannon could see that the ferry was about to dock on the west bank of the swift-moving river. The other door opened just then and the tall man reentered the coach, followed by Oliver Truax.

Sabina Carpenter apparently decided that introductions were in order. Truax had no interest in a drummer of nerve and brain salts, especially one who began the

44

day with a breakfast of straight whiskey; he said, "How do you do," and gave his attention to what was happening outside the coach. The tall man, whose name was Will Coffin and who was the owner and publisher of the *Owyhee Volunteer*, seemed friendlier and more inclined to make conversation.

"These salts of yours, Mr. Lyons," he said bluntly, "are they any good?"

"Excellent. The finest on the market."

"What sort of ills will they cure?"

"Nervous irritability, night sweats, blurring of eyesight, slow circulation of the blood, swollen veins, and weakness of the brain and body as a result of excesses or abuses of any kind."

"Very impressive. How much do they sell for?"

"One dollar the box."

"Perhaps I'll purchase one when we arrive," Coffin said. "I have been under a nervous strain lately."

"Pressures of your profession, Mr. Coffin?"

"Not that so much as the fact that I am being harassed."

"Harassed?"

"By the Chinese population in Silver. Some of them have broken into my house

45

and the newspaper office and destroyed property in both places. God knows what other indignities they've perpetrated in my absence; I've been two days in Boise gathering political news. I asked friends to watch my house and the office, but . . ." He grimaced and shook his head.

"The Chinese are generally a peaceable race where white men are concerned," Quincannon said. "Why have some of them taken after you?"

"Opium," Coffin said.

"Sir?"

"Opium. I have editorialized against the filthy stuff and their open selling of it in no uncertain terms. Do you know what *yenshee* is, Mr. Lyons?"

Quincannon nodded. It was the scrapings of the opium pipe, gathered and saved and sold to addicts who could not afford pure opium; a quarter teaspoon of *yenshee* with a small amount of water sustained the opium-eater's illusion of well-being until his next pipe.

"The worst of them, a merchant named Yum Wing, gives small quantities of it away free — a means to corrupt men and bring him more customers."

"And that ploy has succeeded?"

"All too well. My compositor, Jason

Elder, became an addict that way and has been all but useless at his job since."

"Was Elder a good printer before his addiction?"

"Yes. One of the best I have ever worked with."

Quincannon filed Jason Elder's name away for future consideration.

Oliver Truax said, "There are too many Chinamen in Silver, that's the problem." Now that the stage had come off the ferry and was underway again, he had apparently decided to make himself heard. "The whole lot of them should be run out of town. And Yum Wing and the rest of the elders tarred and feathered first."

"What a quaint idea," Sabina Carpenter said mildly.

Her sarcasm was lost on the fat mine owner. He said, "We would all be better off in that event. And it might happen, too. Mark my words, it well might."

"Vigilante action, Mr. Truax?" she asked.

"If necessary. Wendell McClew is an incompetent buffoon, everyone knows that — the worst town marshal Silver has ever had. He can't control the Chinamen and he can't do anything about the outlaws running loose in the hills, preying on innocent men and women. He can't do *any-*

thing worth a tinker's dam."

"You're being a bit hard on him, Oliver," Coffin said. "McClew isn't as bad as all that."

"I say he is. I say he should be removed from office and a better man installed in his place before the Chinamen run amok."

"Are matters with the Chinese really that serious?" Quincannon asked.

"Hardly," Sabina Carpenter said.

Truax looked at her as if she were a child. "You haven't been in Silver very long, Miss Carpenter. You haven't a proper understanding of the situation."

"But of course you do."

"Of course," Truax said. It was obvious to Quincannon that he was the kind of man who believed in the absolute sanctity of his own viewpoint. It was also obvious to Quincannon that he was an arrogant, pompous, and bigoted troublemaker. "Get rid of the heathens, I say. God-fearing men and women are what we want in Silver City."

"God-fearing *white* men and women," Sabina Carpenter amended.

Truax nodded emphatically. "Just as you say, Miss Carpenter. Just as you say."

They lapsed into silence as the stage rattled on through fertile farmland, the coach jouncing and swaying in its thorough-braces. The movement and the amount of whiskey he had drunk in Nampa gave Quincannon a vicious headache, created more queasiness in his stomach; he sat with his eyes closed, enduring it.

Noon came as they crossed less settled flatland toward the rugged, looming shapes of the Owyhee Mountains. Just before they reached the low foothills that marked the beginning of the Owyhees, they encountered a section of road covered with ruts that ran parallel to each other the width of the coach. The other three passengers had been over this road before; they lowered the side-curtains over the windows as the stage began to crawl through the ruts. Each was full of potholes, some hidden by buildups of powdery dirt; one wheel or another sometimes dropped clear to the hub and caused the coach to jerk and bounce violently, the four of them to hang onto the straps with both hands. Even with the curtains down, the air was clogged with dust. Quincannon had to struggle to keep his sickness down inside him. His head felt as if hobnails were being driven into the inside of his skull.

When they cleared the rutted section the driver stopped and allowed his passengers to rest briefly and compose themselves. Quincannon took the opportunity to drain his flask. The whiskey steadied him again, but added to the pounding in his temples.

Early in the afternoon, well into the lower elevations of the Owyhees, they reached a way station that had been built at a point where two other roads joined the one they had been traveling. The main building was wood-frame, with a covered porch and a sign above it that read: *Poison Creek Station • Meals at All Hours.* At the rear were a large barn and corral. In front was what Coffin referred to as "the big hill"; the road seemed to climb straight up until it disappeared around a curve on the towering mountainside.

"Eight miles from here to Sands Basin and Silver City," Coffin said. "And uphill all the way."

The others ate beans and biscuits inside the station; the sight of the food made Quincannon's stomach jump, and he went back outside to the water pump and washed his face and neck. The rest of his supply of whiskey was in his warbag. He asked the driver, who had just finished putting oats into gunny-sack nose bags for the horses, to get the bag out of the boot for him. When his flask was refilled he had another drink, a small one this time, and judged himself ready to resume the trip.

The uphill trek was slow but not nearly so rough; the road had a natural gravel surface and was less rutted up here. They climbed past basalt bluffs, through stands of juniper and cottonwood and mountain pine, toward granite heights that were partially obscured by low-hanging clouds. Deep canyons fell away below them, some with willow-choked creeks bubbling along their bottoms. The smell of sage that had stayed with them all the way from Nampa was replaced by the spicy scent of juniper. And the air grew cooler as the sun westered and was lost behind the high rocks.

When they neared New York Summit, less than three miles from Silver City, Quincannon could hear dull pounding echoes that he identified even before Truax said, "Powder blasts in the mines. We'll soon be able to hear the stamps as well. It won't be long before our arrival."

Quincannon nodded.

"You'll like our city," Truax assured him, as if he were a member of the Chamber of Commerce. He seemed to have forgotten that Quincannon, at least as far as he knew, was a mere patent medicine drummer. "It's the fastest growing and most progressive in Idaho."

For anyone who doesn't happen to be Chinese, Quincannon thought. He said, "I hope to make many new acquaintances there, Mr. Truax. And to renew an old one."

"Ah? You know someone in Silver, then?"

"A man named Whistling Dixon."

"I don't believe I'm acquainted with anyone by that name."

"I am," Coffin said, "though not personally. He works for one of the cattle ranches at Cow Creek — the Ox-Yoke, I believe." He glanced at Quincannon. "Odd that you should know an old Owyhee cowboy, Mr. Lyons. To the best of my knowledge, Dixon was born in these mountains and has seldom been away from them."

Quincannon said, "My father ranched cattle in Oregon for a time, along the Rogue River, and worked with Dixon there. I was a boy then; Dixon took me under his wing and we became friends. He told me, of course, that he was from this area."

It sounded flimsy in his own ears, but Coffin and Truax seemed to accept the explanation at face value. Sabina Carpenter, however, was watching him curiously

52

again — perhaps even speculatively. A bright woman, Miss Carpenter. And in a way he could not quite define, an odd one too. He wondered just what she was thinking at this moment.

Chapter 4

It was coming on twilight when they arrived in Silver City. The town had been built on the western flank of War Eagle Mountain, a thousand feet below the summit — the highest peak in the Owyhee range, Truax said. It nestled along the upper grade of a deep canyon, cut through by Jordan Creek and full of shadows now, that ran down past smaller and now mostly abandoned mining settlements: Ruby City, Booneville, Wagontown. Mountain peaks rose majestically around Silver, their flanks steep and rocky and supporting few trees; patches of snow still remained in protected spots under the peaks. A saddle coated with gray-green sage and chaparral connected War Eagle with Florida Mountain to the northwest.

Most of the mines were on the sharp-angled slopes of those two peaks. Through the door window, Quincannon could see some of the larger ones built down the side of War Eagle — the long, sweeping angles of their roofs, the fans of faintly luminous white tailings alongside. But while his eyes were on the slopes and on the town ahead, his thoughts were on the drink he would have when they arrived.

They rolled down past a large stage barn, across a railed bridge, and onto a crowded business street that curved up the steep grade of the canyon — "Jordan Street, our main stem," Truax said. The business section appeared to encompass several blocks of Jordan Street and the two immediately parallel to it on either side. Out away from Jordan, the cross streets turned residential. Most of the buildings that stairstepped up the bald, brown hillsides were the high, narrow type common to mining camps; weatherbeaten, constructed in close packs. Lamplight already glowed palely in many of the windows.

As the stage climbed uphill, noise hammered at Quincannon's aching head: the whistle of the hoisting and mill engines, the sullen roar of powder blasts, the tinny throb of saloon music, the rumble of wagons, the cries of animals and the raucous shouts of men. Horses, ore and dray wagons, and private rigs jammed the roadway; people filled the boardwalks. Several of the men wore the garb of cowboys, in for the evening from the nearby ranches. The cattle industry was almost as important in the Owyhee region as mining, Quincannon knew from the government survey pamphlet he'd read in San Francisco. The bare plateau that supported the silver-bearing mountains was carpeted in rich bunchgrass that had drawn stockmen from as far away as Texas.

The driver finally brought the stage to a stop at the Wells Fargo depot. Will Coffin was the first to alight; he helped Sabina Carpenter down. Truax went out next, and as Quincannon followed he saw a woman come forward and embrace the fat mine owner. She was blonde and somewhat Nordic-looking — half Truax's age, half his weight, and twice as pleasing to the eye. But overdressed for a rugged mining town, Quincannon thought, in a silk-and-lace dress and a fancy plumed hat, and carrying a parasol.

"I've missed you, darling," she said. "How was your trip?"

"Fine, fine."

She stepped back a pace, smiled at Truax, and then allowed her gaze to shift to Quincannon as he swung down. Her eyes were light-colored, he noticed; they

56

reminded him of a cat's. "Who is this, Oliver?"

"Eh? Oh, Mr. Lyons. A medicine drummer."

She favored Quincannon with a smile, but it was impersonal and disinterested. Medicine drummers were of no importance to her and therefore not worth her attention.

"This is my wife, Helen," Truax said to Quincannon. Then he laughed and said, "She has no need of your nerve and brain salts, as you can plainly see."

"Indeed I can."

Truax took his wife's arm. "If you'll excuse us, Mr. Lyons. Come along, my dear."

As they moved off, Quincannon turned toward the rear of the stage where the driver was unloading the boot. Sabina Carpenter stood there watching him; had been watching him, he sensed, throughout the brief conversation with the Truaxes. In the twilight the resemblance between her and Katherine Bennett again seemed strong and unsettling. He felt an even sharper need for a drink. The long stage ride had set his nerves on edge.

He waited until Will Coffin had claimed a bulky grip, then took up his own warbag.

57

The newspaperman seemed preoccupied now and had evidently forgotten his earlier interest in Dr. Wallman's Nerve and Brain Salts. Quincannon saw no reason to press him. Coffin tipped his hat to Sabina Carpenter and disappeared into the crowds.

The woman came to Quincannon's side. "My shop is on Avalanche Avenue, between Jordan and Washington," she said. "If you should happen to be interested in a hat during your stay in Silver."

"I doubt that I will be," he said. "I already have a good hat."

"Mine are quite reasonably priced."

"I'm sure they are."

"Well, in any event," she said, "perhaps we'll see each other again before you leave."

"Perhaps. Though I expect most of my time will be occupied."

"In selling salts?"

"That is my job, Miss Carpenter."

"Yes, of course. And I have no doubt that you're adept at it. Good evening, Mr. Lyons."

"Good evening."

He walked downhill toward a sign that said *War Eagle Hotel*. Sabina Carpenter remained in his thoughts. What was the nature of her apparent interest in him? He was a man not unattractive to women; perhaps her boldness stemmed from that. And yet, he felt it was something else, something less personal. It could have nothing to do with his purpose in Silver City — or could it? Depending on where the man named Whistling Dixon led him, he might have to change his mind and visit her millinery shop after all.

At the hotel he registered and dropped off his bag in his room, then went out to the nearest saloon. He drank two whiskeys quickly, nursed a third. The place was jammed with cowpunchers, millhands, mine workers, and their mood was boisterous and friendly; he managed to engage three different men in conversation, confirming from them that Whistling Dixon was, as Coffin had told him, an old Owyhee cowhand some sixty years old. Dixon, whose nickname stemmed from a penchant for constant, tuneless whistling, was neither liked nor disliked; the attitude toward him seemed to be neutral, for the most part because the man kept to himself. He had no family and no friends to speak of, spending his free time either at the Ox-Yoke ranch on Cow Creek, where he worked, or hunting and prospecting in the back country. He came to town no more than once a month, on the average.

There was nothing in any of that to suggest how Dixon might be tied in with a gang of counterfeiters. A false lead after all? Quincannon needed much more information before making a judgment either way.

As for coney coins and greenbacks, a subject he broached carefully, none seemed to have been passed in Silver City. Which added a further point in favor of the boodle game being centered in this area. No smart gang of koniakers would try to shove queer in their own bailiwick; and there was no question that this gang was smart.

Quincannon stopped at two other saloons, this time engaging a variety of townsmen in conversation. Little was known about Sabina Carpenter. She had arrived in Silver City from Denver three weeks ago, opened her millinery shop, and taken up residence at the only boardinghouse in town that catered to women. Although she mingled well and often in local society, she spoke little of personal matters. The consensus seemed to be that she was either a recent widow or a woman retrenching after a bad marriage or an unhappy love affair.

Oliver Truax was one of Silver's wealthy

paragons. He had been a Boise merchant when his brother Amos, who had founded the Paymaster mine, died of congestive heart failure and willed the mine to him. That had been five years ago. Truax ran the Paymaster himself, and within the past year had become dissatisfied with its ore yield and its profits; thus he had formed the Paymaster Mining Company, retained its controlling stock, and opened up the balance of shares to public investors. Apparently most of the money realized from that venture had been put back into the mine, in the form of better equipment and more men to step up production.

Truax often made business trips to Boise, Portland, and Seattle — all cities where large amounts of queer had been shoved, Quincannon noted — and from one such trip to Oregon some ten months ago he had returned with his new young wife. Her background, like Sabina Carpenter's, was murky. And she was not well thought of in town; there were broad hints that she had been unfaithful to her husband with a man named Jack Bogardus, the owner of another smaller silver mine on the south side of War Eagle Mountain, the Rattling Jack. Truax, though he was not actively disliked, was not a popular figure in town — nor among his employees, from whom he demanded hard work and long hours for mediocre wages. Most considered him avaricious, pompous, and a poor blind fool for having married "Helen Roundheels," as one man called her.

Will Coffin had been in Silver three years, having bought the *Volunteer* from its retiring founder in the summer of 1890. Coffin came from Kansas and had a background as a tramp printer and newspaperman. The fact that Coffin himself was a skilled printer interested Quincannon; but he could find out nothing more on that aspect of the man's life.

As for Jason Elder, the *Volunteer*'s part-time compositor, Quincannon also learned little. Elder had worked for Coffin for more than a year, but only sporadically in the past few months as a result of his opium addiction. No one knew where he obtained the money to support his habit. He was a reticent man, one who was regarded with suspicion for that reason, because of his addiction, and because he regularly kept company with Silver City's Chinese population. He lived in a shack at the end of Owyhee Street, on the edge of the Chinese quarter.

There were two schools of opinion as to the competency of Marshal Wendell McClew. The one to which Oliver Truax belonged considered him lazy, slow-witted, and unable or unwilling to cope with Silver's various criminal and communal problems. The other school painted him as a quiet, shrewd lawman who was tough when he had to be and who accomplished as much in his low-key way as any flamboyant peace officer ever could. Both sides seemed to consider him reasonably honest, though the more vehement among his detractors allowed as how they "had reservations" along those lines. The inconclusiveness as to McClew's true nature convinced Quincannon that it would be unwise to reveal his identity and purpose to the marshal, at least at this early stage of his investigation. For all he knew, McClew could be a member of the counterfeiting gang, bought and paid for to provide safety and security in this jurisdiction. No, he would have to play a lone hand for a while, until he gathered more information on a variety of fronts.

It was nearly nine o'clock when he returned to his hotel. He still had no appetite, but the whiskey he had consumed on his rounds had made him woozy and he had no desire for another hangover to-morrow. He forced himself to eat supper in the hotel dining room before retiring. And forbore his usual nightcap when he got into bed.

But for the second night in a row, sleep eluded him — this time because of the dull hammering pulse of the round-the-clock stamp mills, a noise that would take some getting used to. And when he finally did sleep, a long time later, he was plagued by confused dream images of Katherine Bennett that kept mingling with those of Sabina Carpenter, only to be joined by others of his mother. He awoke once, trembling and cold, to the shrill barking of a dog somewhere nearby. In his dream it had sounded like a woman screaming.

An hour past sunup, warmed by his first two drinks of the day, Quincannon left the hotel carrying his sample case. This prom-ised to be a busy day. A talk with Whistling Dixon was indicated, of course, but not just yet. Will Coffin was another he in-tended to see, as was the *Volunteer*'s opium-eating printer, Jason Elder. He also needed to establish his cover identity as a traveling agent for nerve and brain salts, which meant visits to the drugstores in town — a task he would dispose of before giving his attention to the job at hand.

The mountain air was cold, crisp, but the sun had taken the edge off the night's chill. Up the slopes of War Eagle, the mica particles in the long drifts of greenish-white tailings caught the sunlight and made the drifts glisten like new snow. Jordan Street was as crowded as it had been last night, though with a different sort of activity. Ore wagons, empty and laden both, rattled up and down the steep incline, on their way to and from the mines; mingled with them were broughams, buckboards, and freight wagons carrying machinery, produce, hides, scores of other products. Swampers and merchants worked busily at the storefronts, preparing to open their various establishments for the day.

Powder blasts in the mines added rolling thunder echoes to the morning din as Quincannon made his way to the Wells Fargo office, where the Western Union telegrapher was housed. He wrote out a message to Boggs, paid for it, and asked that it be sent immediately. It read:

TO ARTHUR CALDWELL, CALDWELL ASSOCIATES, PHELAN BLDG, SAN FRANCISCO

ARRIVED LAST NIGHT STOP PROS-
PECTS APPEAR GOOD EXCEPT PRIN-
CIPAL YOUR AGE COMMA NATIVE
THIS AREA COMMA AND IN SAME
BUSINESS YOUR NEPHEW CHARLES
STOP WIRE DETAILS SOONEST STOP
DO YOU KNOW TOWN MARSHAL
WENDELL MCCLEW QMK HE MAY BE
OLD FRIEND OF YOURS BUT AM NOT
SURE STOP WILL COMMUNICATE
AGAIN WHEN HAVE NEWS OR HAVE
MADE IMPORTANT SALE

ANDREW LYONS

Boggs' nephew Charles had worked as a cowhand for a variety of cattle ranches in Texas, before a horse threw him one day in 1886 and broke his neck. Boggs would understand the necessity for more information on Whistling Dixon, and step up his own inquiries into the man's background. He would also understand Quincannon's uncertainty about McClew and pursue a line of inquiry into the marshal's background as well.

From the telegrapher Quincannon learned that there were two drugstores operating in Silver and that the nearest was on Washington Street above the courthouse. He went to that one by way of Avalanche Avenue, a deliberate route that took him past Sabina Carpenter's millinery shop. The shop occupied the upper floor of a building above a tonsorial parlor, and was still closed. Most of the other business establishments were already open for the day, including the barber's; he wondered why she had not yet opened hers. It annoyed him that she was a mystery he had so far been unable to solve. Annoyed him, too, that he should be bothered, made uncomfortable by her. That damned resemblance to Katherine Bennett . . .

At the drugstore he spent fifteen minutes convincing the pharmacist to buy six cases of Dr. Wallmann's Nerve and Brain Salts. The man was skeptical at first; he had shelves full of such patent medicines, he said, and had difficulty selling those. Quincannon allowed him to buy the six cases at "a special reduced rate," just so Andrew Lyons could claim the sale.

Outside again, he started down toward the courthouse, with the intention of finding the second drugstore. But he had gone less than half a block when a light spring wagon came clattering out of one of the side streets ahead and veered over to the courthouse. The middle-aged and bespectacled driver brought his horses to a stop near a sign that said JAIL, jumped down, began yelling excitedly, "Marshal! Marshal McClew!" even before he disappeared inside the jail.

From where he stood uphill Quincannon could see into the back of the wagon; a bulky shape wrapped in canvas had been roped to one of the sides. He crossed the street, reached the wagon just as the driver and a tall, mustachioed man wearing a plug hat and a marshals' badge pinned to his cutaway coat came rushing out. The driver was saying, "Found him out in Slaughterhouse Gulch, Marshal. What a sight for a man to come on before breakfast!"

"Shot, you say?"

"See for yourself."

The bespectacled man moved to untie the ropes. Quincannon stepped closer, along with half a dozen others who had been attracted by the brief commotion. The ropes came loose; a stained flap of the canvas was thrown back.

The body inside was that of a man dressed in rough trail garb — a gray-haired, grizzled man of about sixty. His lower jaw had been shot away, but evidently there was still enough of his face intact for identification purposes.

"Well, hell and damn," the plug-hatted man said. "Now who would want to shoot a harmless old waddy like Whistling Dixon?"

Chapter 5

Quincannon moved a step closer to the wagon. The crowd of onlookers had grown; an excited buzzing ran among the men, like the sound of disturbed bees.

The wagon driver said, "Maybe it was robbery. Outlaws all over these mountains, you know that."

Marshal McClew made a snorting noise. "Whistling Dixon never carried more than a dollar in his life, and that's a fact."

"Outlaws don't know it."

"Were you an outlaw, Henry, would you pick him as a target?" McClew ran a thoughtful finger over each of his mustaches. "Found him in Slaughterhouse Gulch, you said. Whereabouts?"

"By that stand of willows where the creek branch runs through. I wouldn't have seen him, back under the trees, except the crows was at him."

"Didn't get his eyes, at least. Sign of his horse?"

"No."

"Anybody else around?"

"Didn't see anybody."

McClew lifted the dead man's arm, let it fall again limply. "Rigor mortis has come and gone," he said. "Been dead a while. Since early last night sometime."

"Bushwhacked, probably. Has to be outlaws, Marshal."

"Maybe," McClew said. "Maybe."

"Well, what you want done with the body?"

"Take it up to Turnbuckle's. I'll go with you. Then we'll notify Doc Petersen, and you can run me out to Slaughterhouse Gulch."

"Me? Hell, I'm already late for work at the livery . . ."

"Can't be helped. I need you to show me just where you found him."

The driver, Henry, climbed grumbling to the wagon seat. McClew started around to the other side, seemed to notice the gathering crowd for the first time, and stopped. "You men — go on about your business. This ain't a public meetingplace. Disperse. Move along!"

Whether he was liked or not, his words

carried weight in Silver City: the crowd immediately began to break up. McClew took his place next to Henry, who snapped the reins and brought his team around and out onto Washington Street. As the wagon rattled away uphill, Quincannon asked one of the men walking near him, "Would Turnbuckle's be an undertaking parlor?"

"It would. Opposite the brewery, two blocks up."

Quincannon walked half a block in that direction, until he came to a saloon. Inside at the plank bar he spent five minutes with a shot of whiskey, timing it by the gold stemwinder his father had given him on his twenty-first birthday. Then he went out again and climbed toward the barnlike building that housed Silver's own brewery, marked by a blackened brick chimney belching smoke.

Opposite the brewery was a squat building with a facade of white-painted fretwork and a sign that read: N.R. TURN-BUCKLE, UNDERTAKER AND CASKET MAKER. The street in front was empty; so was the rutted and weed-choked alleyway that ran alongside. There was no sign of Henry's light spring wagon.

Quincannon ran hard across the street to the undertaking parlor, a ploy to quicken his breathing, and opened the front door to the melody of a little bell. Inside was a hallway and, to one side, a large room with rows of benches and a bier at one end — the place where funeral services were held. A door at the rear of the hall opened momentarily and a small, dapper, balding man emerged and came toward him. Except for his eyes, the man's face was expressionless and might have been molded of soft white clay. The eyes were the saddest Quincannon had ever seen.

"Yes, sir. May I be of service?"

Panting a little, putting gravity and shock into his voice, Quincannon said, "Marshall McClew and Henry, from the livery, just brought you a dead man. Whistling Dixon, by name."

"Why . . . yes, they did. How did you know — ?"

"I happened to be near the jail . . . a tragedy, a dreadful tragedy. My name is Andrew Lyons, from San Francisco. You're Mr. Turnbuckle?"

"Yes, I am. But I don't —"

"Whistling Dixon was a close friend of my father's," Quincannon said, "and a second father to me when I was a boy growing up along the Rogue River. I hadn't seen him in, oh, it must be fifte years. My business brought me to Silver City just last night — I am an agent for Dr. Wallmann's Nerve and Brain Salts, you see — and as I knew Mr. Dixon lived in this area, it was my hope we could renew our friendship after so many years. And now this . . . this tragedy . . . it's most distressing."

Turnbuckle blinked his sad eyes, absorbing what Quincannon had said. Then he murmured, "Of course, Mr. Lyons. A terrible shock for you, I'm sure."

"Terrible," Quincannon repeated. "I wonder . . . I know it's most irregular, but would it be possible for me to see him briefly?"

"See him? Well, I don't —"

"I find it so hard to believe he's dead, murdered. If I could see him for just a minute . . ."

"The body is not pleasant to look at, Mr. Lyons. He was shot, you know, and his face —"

"Violent death has little effect on me," Quincannon said. "I was raised in Indian country, as I said."

Turnbuckle seemed to be weakening. But he said, "The coroner, Dr. Petersen, will be here soon."

"I'll leave as soon as he arrives. A minute

with my poor, murdered friend. That is not too much to ask, is it, Mr. Turnbuckle? Surely?"

"Well, I . . . no, I suppose it isn't . . ."

Quincannon stepped forward and clasped the undertaker's hand, saying, "Thank you, sir, thank you so much," and at the same time turning to him so that they were both moving down the hallway.

Turnbuckle led him to the door at the rear, through it into his workroom. Embalming machinery gleamed in the light from two lamps; so did the undertaker's needles and razors and other tools of his trade, shut away inside glass-fronted cabinets. The unpleasant chemical smell of formaldehyde was strong in the room. Whistling Dixon's corpse lay on a slab in its center, uncovered and faceup, the dead eyes staring at eternity.

"Yes," Quincannon said, "yes, it *is* poor Mr. Dixon."

"Did you doubt it?"

"No, no. I simply find it difficult to believe that such a fine man has been killed in such a terrible fashion. He never carried more than a dollar on his person at any time. Did you know that, Mr. Turnbuckle?"

"I'm afraid I did not have the pleasure of knowing Mr. Dixon."

"Too bad. You would have admired him, just as I did. May I be alone with him for a minute?"

Turnbuckle blinked. "Alone?"

"If you wouldn't mind. I'll soon be leaving Silver City; I may not be here when you've made him ready for burial. I could pay my respects here and now."

"Well, this is most irregular —"

"I realize that. Most irregular. But the circumstances, Mr. Turnbuckle, the circumstances . . . well, you understand."

"Yes," Turnbuckle said uncertainly, "of course."

"A minute is all I ask. No longer."

"Very well, then. A minute, Mr. Lyons, no more."

The undertaker went to the door, glanced back at Quincannon, seemed to shake his head, and went out. Quincannon was already at the slab when the door clicked shut. Quickly he began to search the dead man's clothing.

The shirt pocket contained a nearly empty sack of Bull Durham, papers, and a handful of lucifers. One pocket of a faded and patched Levi jacket was empty; the other yielded a small chunk of ore that Quincannon identified as pyragyrite — the kind of silver ore that contained feldspar,

76

mica flecks, and the reddish, almost crystalline metal known as ruby silver. Nothing unusual in a man, even a cowhand, carrying silver ore in these mountains, he thought; and from what he had learned last night Dixon had done some prospecting in his free time. He returned the chunk to the jacket and went through the pockets of a pair of equally faded and patched Levi's.

A clasp knife with a chipped handle. A silver half eagle that Quincannon held up to catch the lamplight, just long enough to determine that it was not a counterfeit. And a brand-new gold pocket watch, an expensive-looking Elgin with an elaborately scrolled hunting case that depicted a railroad scene. Quincannon flipped open the dustcover, read what was etched on the casing inside.

Jason Elder — 1893.

From the alleyway outside, just as he closed the cover, he heard the sound of a horse and buggy approaching. The Elgin watch went into the pocket of his frock coat, and not a moment too soon: the door to the hallway opened and Turnbuckle came hurrying in.

"I'm sorry, Mr. Lyons," the undertaker said, "but you'll have to leave now. Dr. Petersen is here."

Quincannon sighed. "Of course. I do appreciate your kindness."

"Yes. Now if you will just come with me. . . ."

When they reached the front entrance Quincannon said, "I wonder, Mr. Turnbuckle, if you would allow me to make a small contribution to the burial fund."

Someone had begun to rap on the alley door to the workroom. But Turnbuckle paid no attention to that. His face showed animation again; his ears seemed to prick up like a dog's. "Well," he said, "well, that is hardly necessary, Mr. Lyons. But if you prefer it . . ."

"Oh, I do." Quincannon took a five-dollar note from his billfold and handed it to the undertaker. "You *will* see to it that he has a nice casket, won't you?"

"Oh, indeed. Indeed I will."

Quincannon left Turnbuckle clutching the greenback. It gave him a moment of small, wry amusement to think of what Boggs would say when he encountered an expense labeled "five dollars for Whistling Dixon's burial fund." But it had been money well spent. If Silver City was like other frontier towns, Turnbuckle would receive a fixed sum from city coffers for the burial of men such as Dixon, men without families or estates. Which meant he would be required to itemize any contributions to the burial fund that he received, and to turn the money over to the city — and Turnbuckle had not struck him as the sort of man Diogenes had been searching for with his lantern. The five dollars would disappear. And when it did, any inclination Turnbuckle might have to mention Andrew Lyons' curious visit would disappear along with it.

A pair of brewery wagons, both drawn by thick-bodied dray horses, clogged the street in front of the brewery, waiting to enter the warehouse. The big doors were open and the rich, yeasty smell of beer spiced the air. It made Quincannon thirsty, but it was a thirst he ignored for the moment. The Elgin watch with its fancy case and its inscription was a conscious weight in his pocket.

Why had Whistling Dixon been carrying another man's watch? What was his connection to the opium-smoking tramp printer, Jason Elder?

Chapter 6

The newspaper office was on Volunteer Street, between Jordan and Washington. Through the front window glass, Quincannon could see a man inside at the rear, working at the bulky black shape of a printing press. The mane of hemp-colored hair identified the man as Will Coffin.

Quincannon entered. Coffin glanced over at him, said, "Good morning," in gruff tones, but made no move to leave his labors at the press. He seemed to be alone in the cluttered office, with its two desks and stacks of newsprint and walls framed with past issues of the *Volunteer*. And judging from his tone and from the scowl that twisted his ink-smudged features, he was in a bad humor today.

The press, Quincannon saw as he crossed the office, was an old Albion. Coffin was setting type — taking oily ten-point from the type case on its sloping frames and fitting it into his brass type stick. The smells of printer's ink and oil and newsprint, and the pungent aroma of Coffin's pipe tobacco, were strong in the office.

Quincannon said, "You seem in dark spirits this morning, Mr. Coffin."

"I am, and with good cause. The damned heathens broke in here again while I was in Boise."

"Chinese, you mean?"

"Certainly. Who else would I mean?"

"Was anything stolen?"

"No. But it took me two hours to clean up the results of their mischief." Coffin glowered down at the type stick. "And as if Chinamen running amok aren't trouble enough, I have to do all my own typesetting in order to get the next issue out on time. Damned nuisance all around."

"What about the compositor who sometimes works for you? Jason Elder, is it?"

"Him," Coffin said, as if the word was an epithet. "I went looking for him early this morning; he isn't at that pigsty he lives in and seems not to have been there for days. He is nowhere to be found."

"You have no idea where he might have gone?"

"To hell on his opium pipe, for all I

know or care. Tramp printers! Even at their best, they are notoriously unreliable."

"If you don't mind my saying so, Mr. Coffin, I've heard it mentioned that you yourself were once a tramp printer."

Coffin didn't answer immediately. The type stick was full; he justified the line and then turned to set it in the galley, completing a column. "I was much younger then," he said. "Young men are prone to foolish endeavors. Besides, it was my father's profession — printing, that is. He wasn't a tramp; he owned his own printing and engraving shop in Kansas City for thirty years."

"An expert engraver, was he?" Quincannon asked.

"Yes. He designed his own type face, among other things."

"And you inherited his talent in that area?"

"No, not at all," Coffin said. "I have limited abilities in the printing trade; three years of tramping from Kansas to Montana convinced me of that. Writing copy is a far better occupation than setting it, and a far more suitable one for me."

"I bow to your knowledge of both fields. The only profession I know well, I'm afraid, is patent medicine."

Coffin started to comb fingers through his hair, remembered in time that they were stained with ink, and wiped them on a press rag. He lit an already ink-smeared pipe. When he had it drawing he said, "What brings you here this morning, Mr. Lyons? No takers for your nerve and brain salts?"

"On the contrary, I've already sold six cases to Mr. Judson at the Harmony Drug Store."

"A fruitful morning for you, then."

"So far as business goes," Quincannon said. "Privately, the news is much grimmer."

"Yes, the murder of your friend Whistling Dixon."

"Then you know about that."

"Of course. News travels rapidly in Silver — and bad news reaches my door sooner than most. I suppose you're wondering why I'm here setting type instead of out gathering information."

"I am, yes."

"I've owned the *Volunteer* three years and never missed a single Wednesday's publication," Coffin said. "It is a matter of pride with me. If I don't spend the rest of today and most of tonight right here in the office, there will be no paper tomorrow."

Quincannon asked, "But have you spoken to the marshal? Do you have any further details?"

"Is that why you've come, Mr. Lyons? Seeking information on Dixon's murder?"

"Yes."

"Well, I'm afraid I can't help you. I haven't spoken to Marshal McClew yet and I expect I know nothing more about Dixon's death than you. And I won't until McClew comes to see me later today. He always does in such matters, just in time for me to write my story. He enjoys seeing his name in print."

"I've heard that the Owyhees are a haven for outlaws," Quincannon said. "Is murder common in Silver City?"

"Not uncommon, shall we say. And that is another reason I'm here and not out with McClew. Murder, unless it happens to be of the spectacular variety, has limited news value."

"Yes — the shooting of a cowhand can hardly be called spectacular, can it?"

"Frankly, no. If that fact offends you, so be it."

Coffin picked up a page proof he had already run off, scanned it, frowned, and then turned to one of the galleys. Quincannon watched him plug a dutchman in a poorly spaced ad, then asked, "Were you well acquainted with Dixon?"

"I barely knew him," Coffin answered. "I spoke to him perhaps twice in the three years I've been in Silver."

"Do you know of any friends he might have in town?"

"No."

"Was he acquainted with Jason Elder?"

Coffin squinted at him through smoke from his pipe. "What makes you ask that?"

"Dixon was murdered and Elder seems to have disappeared. Perhaps there's some connection."

"I find that unlikely. As far as I know, Elder and Dixon never met."

"Tell me this: If Elder worked for you only occasionally in recent weeks, how was he able to support his opium habit?"

Coffin scowled; he had grown weary of all the questions. He said, "I have no idea. Nor do I care. Now if you will excuse me, Mr. Lyons, I have four more pages of type to set and an editorial to write."

Quincannon left the newspaper office, went to Jordan Street and uphill along it. He wondered if Marshal McClew had found out anything important in Slaughterhouse Gulch. But that was unlikely, if Whistling Dixon had been murdered by the gang of koniakers; they were too disciplined to leave obvious traces of themselves at the scene of a fatal shooting. Still, should he talk to McClew anyway? He decided against it. Perhaps later, but not just yet.

Thinking was a chore, out here with the rumbling wagons and the constant noise from the mines; he let his mind go blank as he continued climbing to the upper reaches of Jordan Street. The buildings clustered up there were little more than shacks, some of them made of tarpaper and hammer-flattened tin cans — the Chinese quarter. Yellow faces replaced white; coolie outfits and straw hats replaced the conventional garb of the mining camp. Two middle-aged Chinese came down the slope toward him, both with wooden "yokes of servitude" across their shoulders, five-gallon water cans balanced on each end. Aside from the digging of ditches and the building of roads, one of the few jobs open to Chinese in these mountains would be delivering water from door to door for a few cents a day. Even more demeaning were the other tasks for which the yoke would be used: to carry slop for the hogs and buckets for the cleaning of white men's privys.

Near where Jordan Street petered out against the steep mountainside, Quincannon spied a small business section: a handful of stores, a pair of joss houses, some kind of meeting hall made of heavily weathered clapboard. He went along there, looking at each of the buildings. All were marked with Chinese characters; only one bore any English lettering, but that was the one he was interested in. A small sign to one side of a door hinged with strips of cowhide said GENERAL STORE, and below that, in smaller lettering, YUM WING, PROPRIETOR.

Quincannon pushed open the door and stepped into the dark, windowless interior. The mingled scents of herbs and spices and burning joss sticks assailed him. He paused to allow his eyes to adjust to the murky light. At first he thought the store was deserted; then he realized that a man was standing motionless behind a long plank counter. The man did not move or speak as Quincannon crossed among tables laden with Chinese clothing, past shelves of pots and pans, tea, medicinal herbs and other, unrecognizable items.

The Chinese, Quincannon saw when he reached the plank, was fat and middle-aged, with a graying wisp of mustache and his hair braided into a long queue down his back. He stood with his arms folded and his hands hidden inside the sleeves of his black coolie jacket — an aging Buddha surveying a temple of his own construction.

Quincannon said, "Yum Wing?"

A small bow. "How may I serve you?"

"I'm looking for a customer of yours, a white man named Jason Elder."

Yum Wing's round, smooth face might have been a mask for all it revealed. "Why does your search bring you to me?" he asked. He spoke English precisely, with much less accent than most frontier Chinese. An educated man, Quincannon thought. And a dangerous one, if his eyes and his demeanor were accurate indicators.

"Elder was a good customer, wasn't he?"

"Many *fan quai* are good customers of my humble shop."

Fan quai. Foreigners — foreign devils. Quincannon had worked among the Chinese in San Francisco; he was familiar with their language. And familiar with men such as Yum Wing, men who hated Caucasians, who pretended to be subservient to the white race while cheating and plotting against them at every opportunity. Yes: Yum Wing was a dangerous man.

Quincannon said, *"Yo yang-yow mayo?"*

If Yum Wing was surprised that Quincannon spoke his language, he gave no sign of it. "I have opium for sale, yes," he said in English. "Very fine opium, from Shanghai."

"Elder bought it from you, is that right?"

"I have many customers for my opium."

"How much do you charge?"

"Enough for one pill, two bits."

"You have *yenshee*, too?"

"Very fine *yenshee*. One ounce, one dollar."

"How much opium a day did you sell Jason Elder?"

Silence.

"How much *yenshee?*"

Silence.

"Where did he get the money to pay you?"

Silence.

"When did you last see him?"

"You will purchase opium? *Yenshee?*"

"If you tell me where I can find Elder."

A small shrug. "I have not seen him in four days."

"Did he say anything then about leaving Silver City?"

"I am only a humble Chinese merchant," Yum Wing said. "Not worthy of such confidences."

"Have you any idea where he went?"

"I have no idea. I have goods for sale. Very fine goods, very fine opium."

"Will Coffin, the newspaper editor, doesn't think so."

Silence.

"You've had trouble with Coffin, haven't you?"

"No trouble. China boys avoid trouble with white men."

"Not always. Sometimes they have cause not to avoid it."

Silence.

It was pointless to continue, Quincannon decided. Yum Wing would not admit to even knowing Will Coffin. And if he knew why Jason Elder had disappeared, or where Elder was now, he would not admit that either.

Quincannon said, "Will Coffin isn't your true enemy, Yum Wing. Greed and hate are." He turned and moved away through the dark, cramped, silent room, out into the sunlight and the throbbing noise from the stamp mills.

Owyhee Street was a short distance away: he found it without difficulty. It curled up one of the bare hillsides, petered out near a wood-and-tarpaper shack that had been built at an odd angle against a shelf of rock, so that its entrance was hidden from the road. This was the shack that Jason Elder occupied, according to what Quincannon had learned on his saloon rounds last night.

A beaten-down path led through a section of dry sage and weeds that separated the shack from the street. Two crabapple trees grew alongside the dwelling, shading it and further concealing its entrance. The single facing window, Quincannon saw as he passed under the trees, was glassless and covered with crude wooden shutters. Tacked onto the front wall was a rickety porch of sorts; he stepped up onto it, reached for the door latch.

It jerked inward in that same instant. And someone came hurrying out and ran right into him.

The collision threw them both off balance, knocked something loose from the other's hand and sent it flying out into the dry grass. Quincannon blindly caught hold of the person's clothing to steady them both; felt flesh under it that was soft, rounded — distinctly feminine. Hands slapped away his hands, shoved him back.

He was looking into the startled and angry face of Sabina Carpenter.

Chapter 7

She was wearing a plain skirt today, with a buckskin jacket over a white shirtwaist, and her dark hair was mostly hidden by a Portland-style straw hat. No reticule, which struck Quincannon as odd: it was his experience that women seldom went anywhere without a bag, unless they had a good reason. Two spots of color glowed on her cheeks; she rubbed at one as if to make the color disappear. "My God," she said, "you frightened me half to death. What are you doing here?"

"I might ask you the same thing."

She made no reply. She was peering out to one side of him, at where the object that had been in her hand lay on the ground. He followed the direction of her gaze, saw that the object was a fold of heavy parchment paper; he moved at the same time she did so that he blocked her way with his body and reached the paper first.

Sabina Carpenter said angrily, "Give me that," and tried to pull it from his grasp. Quincannon held her away, unfolding the paper with his free hand so he could determine what it was. A stock certificate — two hundred and fifty shares in Oliver Truax's Paymaster Mining Company. It had been made out in the name of Helen Truax, but on the reverse side, Quincannon saw just before Sabina Carpenter kicked him and then wrenched the certificate away, was Helen Truax's endorsement and Jason Elder's name as the new owner of the stock.

Her breath coming rapidly now, the Carpenter woman had backed off a few paces clutching the certificate. There was a wary tenseness in her, but no apparent fear. If he moved toward her, Quincannon thought, she wouldn't turn and flee, as most women would in such a situation; she would stand her ground and fight him.

He said mildly, "Thievery, Miss Carpenter?"

"Of course not."

"That certificate has two names on it, neither of them yours."

"It was lying on the floor inside," she said. "Mr. Elder isn't home and I thought . . . well, it seems valuable. I intend to take it to the marshal for safe-keeping."

"Why not return it to Mrs. Truax?"

She hesitated before she said, "It belongs to Mr. Elder now. Besides, I hardly know the woman."

"Elder must know her quite well, to be the recipient of such a large amount of stock."

"I couldn't say."

"And you must know Elder quite well yourself, to be inside his house alone."

"Your innuendoes are offensive, Mr. Lyons," she said stiffly. "I know Mr. Elder no better than I know Mrs. Truax. I came to see him about a hat he ordered. The door was open, so I simply walked inside."

She was lying, Quincannon thought, making up her answers out of whole cloth. He said, "Then you aren't aware that Elder has been missing for four days."

"Missing? How do you know that?"

"Will Coffin told me."

"I see. And why are *you* here, then?"

"Whistling Dixon. You've heard about his murder, haven't you?"

"Murder?" Her surprise, at least, seemed genuine. "No, I hadn't heard."

"Yes. And I've learned that Dixon and

Elder were acquainted. Were you aware of that?"

She shook her head. "I told you, I hardly know Jason Elder. And I did not know Whistling Dixon at all."

He studied her for a time, and received the same sort of scrutiny in return. He felt stirred by her again, by her resemblance to Katherine Bennett and by her odd actions and by some intangible quality that he could not quite define. Uneasiness formed in him, made him yearn for a drink of whiskey.

At length she said, "I'll be on my way now, Mr. Lyons. If you believe me guilty of wrongdoing, perhaps you would like to accompany me to the marshal's office."

"That won't be necessary," he said, and saw relief flicker in her eyes. She had no intention of taking the stock certificate to Marshal McClew, he thought. But what did she want with it?

Blackmail or extortion — was either of those her game?

She turned away from him and went along the path, around under the crabapple trees. Quincannon moved to the corner and watched her reach Owyhee Street, hurry down it toward Jordan. When she was out of sight he returned to the porch and entered the shack.

It was a single room, not clean and sparsely furnished. From the look of it, Jason Elder either lived in a state of upheaval — the "pigsty" Will Coffin had referred to — or the shack had been searched thoroughly and rather recklessly. Quincannon was inclined toward the latter theory, with Sabina Carpenter as the most obvious culprit.

A cot had been upended in one corner; a pair of filthy blankets were wadded nearby, along with a torn or slashed pillow leaking feathers onto the packed-earth floor. A flat-topped trunk, old and disreputable, stood with its lid up, some of its contents still inside and the rest spilled out around it. A chair lay on its side next to a small table. Pots, pans, two broken dishes, a tin basin, and a straight razor were also scattered about; and against one wall, a canister of flour and another of sugar lay upended, their contents mingled like a sifting of snow and acrawl with insects. The only items in the room that seemed to still be in their proper place were an ancient sheet-iron stove, its door hinged open, and an empty woodbox.

On one wall shelf was a black-lacquered Chinese tray; Quincannon crossed to look at it. It contained the instruments of Jason Elder's opium addiction: the *toy,* a small bone box that held the opium; the *yen hok* needle on which the pill was cooked; a little oil lamp; the sponge known as the *souey pow;* an enamel cup to hold the *yenshee;* the slender ivory tube, not quite two feet long, that was the stem of the pipe; and the round, crusted black bowl, the size of a doorknob, with its tiny center hole. He picked up the *toy,* looked inside, and found that it contained a small amount of raw opium. And when he examined the *yenshee* cup he saw that at least a quarter of an ounce of the black scrapings lay within.

Everything was here, all the keys that would unlock the gateway to celestial dreams — keys that no opium addict would willingly leave behind. Wherever Elder had gone, circumstances must have forced him to leave in a great hurry, from some location other than this shack. Either that, or someone else had been responsible for his disappearance.

Quincannon examined the contents of the flat-topped trunk. Shirts, a pair of trousers, galluses, stockings, underdrawers, a pair of crumbling books on the printing trade in general and various type faces in particular, and an empty carpetbag —

most if not all of Elder's personal possessions. None of it contained any clues to his present whereabouts, to his connection with Whistling Dixon or Helen Truax or Sabina Carpenter. Nor was there anything that even hinted that Elder might be involved with the koniakers.

The remainder of the room likewise revealed nothing of interest. If any other unusual item aside from the stock certificate had once been kept here, Sabina Carpenter — or another party; Will Coffin, for one, had also been to the shack — had made off with it.

Quincannon went outside, back to Owyhee Street and then down Jordan. The first saloon he came to drew him inside and held him for ten minutes, the time it took to drink two whiskeys to ease his mind and eat a sandwich and two pickled eggs to ease the hunger pangs in his stomach. Then, following directions he had obtained from the bartender, he found his way to the house where the Truaxes lived, east across Jordan Creek on a hummock that overlooked most of the town and descending valley beyond.

The house differed considerably in style from most of the buildings in Silver City — a bastardized Italianate with a single jutting cupola and an ornate front veranda bordered by lilac bushes. No doubt the fanciest home in Silver, Quincannon judged; he would have been surprised, having met both Oliver Truax and his wife, if it had been otherwise. He climbed to the veranda, pulled the ring for the bell.

No one responded to the summons. Helen Truax was out somewhere, perhaps shopping; he would have to wait until later to talk to her.

From the Truax house he went to the Wells Fargo office, where he wrote out another Western Union telegram to be sent to Boggs in care of the "Caldwell Associates" mail-drop in San Francisco. This one read:

PRINCIPLE ACCOUNT BANKRUPT NO EXPLANATION YET STOP HAVE SEVERAL OTHER POSSIBILITIES TO INDICATE THIS IS FRUITFUL TERRITORY STOP WILL COFFIN FROM KANSAS CITY OWNER LOCAL NEWSPAPER HAS BEEN MOST HELPFUL SO HAVE OLIVER TRUAX OWNER PAYMASTER MINE AND WIFE HELEN STOP REMEMBER SABINA CARPENTER FROM DENVER QMK SHE IS HERE AND VERY ACTIVE

All of which would tell Boggs that Whistling Dixon had been killed, that his death might be connected with the counterfeiting operation, and that Quincannon required information on Will Coffin, the Truaxes, and especially Sabina Carpenter.

He remained at the Western Union counter until the brass pounder had sent the message. Leaving then, he located Cadmon's Livery near the stage barn. The hostler turned out to be the bespectacled man named Henry who had found Whistling Dixon's corpse; Quincannon mentioned the murder and then asked, with apparent casual curiosity, if Marshal McClew had found anything in Slaughterhouse Gulch that might identify the killers.

Henry said that he hadn't. "And he likely never will, either," he added. "Outlaws done it. Damned few of those sons of bitches ever get caught. They don't hang around Silver long enough for that, once they rob or kill somebody."

Quincannon rented a horse — a blaze-faced roan with four white stockings — and then asked Henry how to get to the Paymaster mine. He rode out of town on a rutted wagon road that led up the face of War Eagle Mountain. Ore wagons rolled past him, on their way to and from the mines; the thud and boom of the stamps and powder blasts seemed to grow louder, hollower as he climbed toward the tiered buildings above. The high country wind blew cool against his face, made him feel almost chilly.

So did the nagging mental image of Sabina Carpenter, unwanted, vexing, like a splinter that had worked its way deep into his flesh and would not come out.

Chapter 8

The buildings of the Paymaster mine were arranged on tiers down the mountainside, so that they resembled a single multilevel structure. Their sheet-metal roofs glistened under the afternoon sun. So did the fan of tailings below the stamp mill, spread out from the foot of the cantilevered tramway that extended down to the mill from the main tunnel above.

Quincannon rode into the mine yard. Three men were harnessing a team of dray horses to a big, yellow-painted Studebaker freight wagon; the only other men in sight were up on the tram, pushing ore carts from the tunnel to the chute that fed the mill, back again for another load. Quincannon dismounted, tied the roan to one of the yard stanchions, and approached the men at the Studebaker wagon to ask the location of the mine office.

One of the men pointed to a small

building upslope. "But if you're looking for Mr. Truax," he said, "he ain't there."

"Where would I find him?"

"Down in the mill. Stairs over yonder."

A dynamite explosion deep inside the mine made the ground tremble as Quincannon descended a steep flight of stairs to the stamp mill. When he entered he had no trouble locating Truax; together with a burly man in miner's garb, probably the mill foreman, he was inspecting one of the eccentrics that raised the stamps, shut down now and locked into place. Rather than interrupt them, Quincannon stayed where he was near the entrance and watched the machinery and the millhands at their work.

He had visited a stamp mill once before, in the Comstock Lode; he knew how they worked. The smaller pieces of ore that came tumbling down the chute went through a three-inch grizzly or grating into the feed bins; anything larger was shunted into a jaw crusher. The dressed ore was fed automatically to the stamps, where it was wet-stamped with a mixture of mercury, water, and patio reagents; the mercury drew the raw silver out of the slimes. At the end of a long process that included mulling, separating, and drainage, slugs of amalgam emerged and were delivered to retort furnaces that distilled off the quicksilver. The sponge matte was then melted and cast into bars in the adjacent melting room.

Quincannon waited ten minutes in the lanternlit enclosure, keeping out of the way of the sweating millhands, before Truax and his foreman finished their inspection and the fat mine owner turned toward the entrance. Truax recognized Quincannon with no outward show of surprise. He gestured that they go outside, where they could make themselves heard above the thunder of the iron-shod stamps.

"Well, Mr. Lyons, what brings you here?"

"A private matter," Quincannon said. "I wonder if we might talk in your office?"

"I'm a busy man, you know. If it concerns salts or whatever it is you're selling . . ."

"Not at all. It concerns buying, not selling."

"Ah? Buying what?"

"Shares in the Paymaster Mining Company, perhaps, if they're available."

Truax's expression changed; an avid sort of interest shone in his eyes. "Well, then, I'm sure I can spare you a few minutes.

Yes, I'm sure I can. Come along, Mr. Lyons."

He led the way up the stairs. The workers who had been harnessing the drays to the Studebaker wagon were gone now, but two other men had taken their place. One was dressed in standard miner's clothing; the other, swarthy and half a head taller, wore a frock coat over gray twill trousers, and a Montana peaked hat. When the tall one spied Truax he came quickly away from the wagon.

Truax said, "Hello, Bogardus," without enthusiasm. The tone of his voice and the look on his face told Quincannon that the swarthy man was not someone he liked.

Quincannon wondered if that was because of the rumors he'd heard about Jack Bogardus and Truax's wife. He studied the owner of the Rattling Jack mine, who had acknowledged Truax's greeting with a curt nod and was now staring at the man with thinly veiled hostility. He was about forty, clean-shaven except for thick sideburns, with a long dark face and the eyes of a hellfire preacher. Some women would find him attractive, Quincannon thought; those fiery eyes had a spellbinding quality.

"The wagon and team are ready for you," Truax said, "as you've no doubt seen. Did you bring the cash?"

"Would I be here if I hadn't?"

"Come along to the office."

But Bogardus didn't move. "One of those horses is spavined," he said.

"Nonsense."

"Right hock on the big gray. Look at it yourself."

"I don't need to look at it. Those horses are sound; so is the wagon. The price is five hundred, Bogardus, just as we agreed on. Not a penny less."

Bogardus showed his teeth in a sardonic smile. "If I didn't need that wagon I'd tell you to go to hell."

"But you do need it, so you say. And no one else in Silver has one for sale. Besides, you can afford my price, now that you've struck your new vein."

"A richer vein than you ever saw," Bogardus said.

"Indeed? I find that difficult to believe."

"I don't give a damn what you believe, Truax."

"My time is valuable and you're wasting it. I have business to discuss with this gentleman." He nodded at Quincannon. "Five hundred cash, Bogardus. Will you pay it?"

Bogardus produced a money clip that

held a thick sheaf of notes. From it he removed five one-hundred-dollar greenbacks. His fiery eyes remained fixed on Truax's face; Quincannon might not have been there at all. "You'll get these when I have a bill of sale," he said.

"Don't you trust me?"

"No more than you trust me."

Truax made a laughing sound that had no mirth in it. He set out upslope; Bogardus stared after him for a moment and then followed, and Quincannon did the same. Inside the mine office Truax clumped past a man seated at a high desk piled with ledgers, went through a doorway into a private office, and sat down at a polished cherrywood desk that was much too ornate to have been made in Silver City. Neither Bogardus nor Quincannon shut the door when they entered. Bogardus slapped the five hundred-dollar notes on the desktop, kept his hand on them until Truax had written out a bill of sale and signed it and Bogardus had read it over. Truax added the greenbacks to others in a silver clip of his own; Bogardus put the bill of sale away inside his frock coat. Not a word was spoken through all of this, nor after the transaction was finished. The two men exchanged a final look, after which

Bogardus turned on his heel and stalked out.

Quincannon closed the door and occupied a chair opposite Truax. "I take it you and Mr. Bogardus aren't friends," he said.

"Friends? The man is a scoundrel and worse."

"How so, Mr. Truax?"

"For one thing, he is a fornicator. I cannot abide a fornicator."

So Truax did know, or at least suspect, that his wife might be cuckolding him with Bogardus. Quincannon asked, "Is he also dishonest?"

"He is. Dishonesty is how he obtained his Rattling Jack mine two years ago."

"Oh? A swindle?"

"Not precisely. The former owner, Jack Finkle, had it up for sale because of failing health — asking a fair price, I might add. Bogardus arranged two accidents at the mine, one that crippled Finkle's son-in-law, in order to drive the selling price down to where he could afford it. Everyone knows it was his work, but nothing was ever proved."

"The Rattling Jack is a well-paying mine, then?"

"It wasn't until Bogardus struck a new vein six months ago. The old vein was

108

gradually pinching out." Truax's voice was bitter; it was plain that he begrudged Bogardus his newfound wealth. "Now his ore is assaying at one hundred dollars a ton, so he claims. Half of what the Paymaster assays at twice the tonnage per day, but still substantial."

"Is that why he needs a new freight wagon? To ship more of his silver?"

"Evidently. He lost his biggest wagon last week, I'm told; one of his drivers misjudged a turn coming down the pass road, his load shifted, and the wagon went over the side." Truax said that last with satisfaction.

Quincannon asked, "Is Bogardus a native of Silver City?"

"No. Came here a few months before he purchased the Rattling Jack."

"From where?"

"Somewhere in Oregon." Truax frowned. "You seem unduly interested in Bogardus, Mr. Lyons."

Quincannon smiled disarmingly. "Idle curiosity," he said. "I fear I have an inquisitive nature."

"Indeed." Truax opened a humidor on his desk, took out an expensive cheroot, sniffed it, then picked up a pair of silver clippers and snipped off the end. He did not offer Quincannon one of the cigars. "Now then," he said, when he had the cheroot burning to his satisfaction, "you wanted to discuss the purchase of Paymaster stock?"

"Yes. Are shares available?"

"Possibly. But you'll pardon me, Mr. Lyons, if I ask how a patent medicine drummer can expect to buy valuable shares in one of the largest and most profitable silver mines in the state of Idaho."

"Oh, it's not I who is interested in purchasing the shares," Quincannon said. "No, I am inquiring on behalf of the president of my company, Mr. Arthur Caldwell of San Francisco. You've heard of him, surely?"

"No, I can't say that I have."

"A very important man," Quincannon said. "He is a close friend of Mr. Charles Crocker, among others."

Truax had heard of Crocker, one of the "Big Four" railroad tycoons who had been potent factors in the shaping of California politics and economy for close to thirty years; and the name impressed him. Interest glittered in his eyes again, ignited by what Quincannon took to be the spark of greed. "Mr. Caldwell is well-to-do, then?" he asked.

"Extremely. Stock speculation is both a hobby and an avocation with him; he has been quite successful."

"Am I to understand that you act as his agent in such matters?"

"No, not at all. I am merely a patent medicine drummer, as you pointed out, although I do have ambitions, of course. I have scouted likely stock prospects for Mr. Caldwell in the past, and he has seen fit to reward my help with cash bonuses. I expect I will also soon be promoted to a managerial position with our San Francisco office."

"I see," Truax said. He waved away a cloud of fragrant smoke. "And you feel the Paymaster Mining Company would be a good investment for him?"

"I do, based on inquiries I made in town this morning. I spoke to Sabina Carpenter, for one. She told me she recently purchased an amount of Paymaster stock."

"Yes, that's correct. Five thousand dollars' worth."

Quincannon raised an eyebrow. "That's quite a substantial investment for the owner of a millinery shop."

"An inheritance from an aunt in Denver, I believe."

"Ah, I see," Quincannon said. But he

was wondering if that was really where Sabina Carpenter had obtained the five thousand dollars. "Can you tell me how much stock is available for purchase by Mr. Caldwell?"

"Well, the original issue was twenty-five thousand shares, nearly all of which has been sold. I'll have to check to determine just how much is left. However, I can tell you now that one of our large Seattle stockholders has expressed a willingness to sell at the right price."

"How many shares does this stockholder control?"

"Let me see . . . two thousand, I believe."

"Do you know how much he would be willing to take for them?"

"He has said he would accept fifty dollars a share. Fair market value, I assure you."

"You yourself own controlling stock in the company, I take it — you and your charming wife."

"I do, yes," Truax said. "Ten thousand shares. But the stock is in my name alone."

"Mrs. Truax has none at all?"

"No. Well, I gifted her with two hundred and fifty shares as a wedding present, but that is hardly a significant amount."

"Do any of the other major stockholders live in Silver City?" Quincannon asked.

"No. They are all scattered throughout Idaho, Oregon, Washington, and California."

Quincannon sat in speculative silence for a time. Truax, who seemed to be trying to contain his eagerness, took the opportunity to fetch up a bottle of Kentucky sour mash from a sideboard behind his desk.

"Drink, Mr. Lyons?"

"Well . . . I don't mind if I do."

Truax poured one for each of them. Quincannon drank his without savoring or even tasting it; except for its low heat in his throat and stomach, it might have been bootleg hooch made out of tobacco and wood alcohol.

Truax said in greasy tones, "May I count on you to recommend the Paymaster Mining Company to Mr. Caldwell?"

"I will recommend that he consider it, yes."

"Excellent."

"He will make inquiries of his own, naturally," Quincannon said. "And if he does decide to buy, I'm sure he'll contact you directly."

"I shall be delighted to hear from him." Quincannon made as if to vacate his chair, and Truax said, as Quincannon had hoped he would, "Another drink before you leave?"

"Yes, thanks. Kind of you."

He made the second whiskey last for two swallows. Then he stood and shook hands with Truax, who remained seated. "Perhaps we'll see each other again before I leave Silver City, Mr. Truax," he said.

"It would be a pleasure. Will you be staying long?"

"Not as long as I had expected." Quincannon assumed a solemn expression. "The old friend I had hoped to see, Whistling Dixon, was killed last night."

Truax's reaction was nil, beyond a look of sympathy as feigned as Quincannon's grief. If anything, he seemed disinterested — but that may have been feigned, too. "What happened to the poor fellow?"

"No one knows exactly. He was shot sometime last night, in Slaughterhouse Gulch."

"Shot?"

"Murdered."

"Bandits," Truax said immediately. "These mountains are acrawl with them."

"Yes, so I've been told." Quincannon shook his head. "It seems to be a day for unpleasant news," he said. "I spoke to Will

114

Coffin this morning; he told me the newspaper office was broken into again during his absence."

Truax showed no particular interest in that either. "Was there much damage?"

"Little enough."

"Those damned heathen Chinamen ought to be run clear out of the Owyhees."

"So you said yesterday," Quincannon reminded him blandly. "Poor Mr. Coffin. To compound his problems, his part-time printer, Jason Elder, has disappeared."

"Elder? Oh yes, the opium addict."

"You don't know the man personally?"

"Of course not. I don't keep company with dope fiends."

Perhaps not, Quincannon thought, but your wife surely does. He said, "Well, I won't take up any more of your time, Mr. Truax. Thank you for seeing me, and for your excellent whiskey."

"Not at all. My pleasure. Ah, you will be sending a wire to Mr. Caldwell right away, won't you?"

"This very evening."

"Will you let me know if you have a reply from him?"

"Right away."

Truax beamed at him. He even stood up as Quincannon took his leave of the office.

Riding out of the mine yard, Quincannon fired his pipe and reflected sourly that he was accumulating a great deal of curious information but that none of it seemed to fit together into a useful pattern. Nor did any of it seem directly related to the gang of koniakers, with the probable exception of Whistling Dixon's murder and the possible exception of Jason Elder's disappearance. And now he needed the answers to several puzzling and related questions before he could even begin to piece things together.

Why had Helen Truax signed over all of her two hundred and fifty shares in the Paymaster Mining Company to Elder — shares worth better than twelve thousand dollars?

Why had Sabina Carpenter taken those shares from Elder's shack and what did she intend to do with them?

Why was Truax so eager to sell Paymaster stock?

What, exactly, was Helen Truax's relationship with Jack Bogardus?

And if Bogardus was as dishonest as Truax claimed, did that dishonesty extend to counterfeiting and murder?

Chapter 9

When he arrived back in town Quincannon went directly to the Western Union desk at the Wells Fargo office. It was too early to expect answers to his wires, but there was always the chance that Boggs had news of his own to impart. He found nothing for him when he arrived, however. He sent Boggs another wire care of Caldwell Associates, this one requesting information on Jack Bogardus, and then returned his rented horse to the livery and walked back up to the War Eagle Hotel.

In his room he lay on the bed and cudgeled his brain for an hour, without much consequence. Restlessness and hunger drove him out again. He ate a small meal at a cafe nearby, and when he was done it was early evening and the saloons were beginning to fill up with cowhands, miners, and townsmen. He did as he had done the previous night: drifted from saloon to saloon, taking a drink in each, engaging this man and that in apparently idle conversation.

The murder of Whistling Dixon was a favorite topic, but Quincannon picked up no new information or useful speculation on the shooting. He did learn that although Dixon had no real friends among the Ox-Yoke cowboys, he had most often partnered with a waddy named Sudden Wheeler; and that if anyone had known Dixon and his private ways, it was Wheeler. Quincannon had already planned to ride out to the Ox-Yoke tomorrow. Now that he had Wheeler's name, it might simplify his inquiries.

Information was meager on other fronts as well. As far as any of the miners who worked at the Paymaster knew, the mine was still producing high-grade ore on the same steady basis as in previous years. The payload vein wouldn't last forever, as one miner said, and it wasn't as rich as it had been in the seventies, but he wasn't worrying about his job. That being the case, it was unlikely that Truax's eagerness to sell Paymaster stock stemmed from an urgent need for money — at least as far as the mine itself went. Any other motives he might have were well hidden.

Jack Bogardus was generally disliked in Silver, though not with the vehemence Truax had exhibited. The consensus seemed to be that he had obtained the Rattling Jack mine through dishonest methods, as Truax had claimed. He had been an abrasive sort to deal with personally and professionally up until his discovery of the rich new vein; since then he had mended his ways somewhat, lost his public contentiousness, and modified his penchant for petty conniving. Now he was tolerated, especially in saloon circles; when he was in town for reasons other than Helen Truax, which wasn't often, he stood drinks for the house.

He was secretive about the Rattling Jack's new vein; he had built a stockade around the mine compound and allowed no one inside except the dozen or so men who worked for him. Quincannon found this secrecy of potential interest. Perhaps the man was only being overly protective of his holdings; but a fence might also mean that he had something to hide. It was a fact to be looked into more closely.

Questions about Jason Elder netted him nothing more than he already knew. Questions about the Chinese population in general and Yum Wing in particular were likewise unproductive. Aside from the usual prejudice against the Chinese, there was little animosity such as Truax and Coffin had demonstrated. The yellow men were tolerated in much the same way Bogardus was tolerated, and that included Yum Wing and his opium peddling. A few of the men Quincannon spoke to even seemed surprised that Will Coffin was being harassed. "Hell," one man said, "them Chinamen is a peaceable bunch. Seems to me it'd take a lot more than a couple of editorials to stir 'em up to busting into Coffin's house and the newspaper office."

Quincannon, from his personal knowledge of the Chinese race, agreed with that assessment. It was something that had been bothering him. Either trouble ran deep and dark between Coffin and the Orientals of Silver City, or somebody else was responsible for the break-ins. The same person or persons who had ransacked Jason Elder's shack, for instance.

Sabina Carpenter?

Looking for what?

When Quincannon left the sixth saloon he was feeling the effects of the whiskey, starting to lose his clearheadedness. It was dark now and the gas lamps had been lighted along Jordan and along the narrow winding streets that climbed the hillsides to the east and west. The night wind blowing down off War Eagle Mountain was chill; he walked into the teeth of it, to chase away the muzziness from the liquor.

On impulse he turned west on Avalanche Avenue, toward Sabina Carpenter's millinery shop. He expected to find it dark, but it wasn't; lamplight illuminated the second-floor window and the words painted on it: SABINA'S MILLINERY • FINE HATS FOR LADIES AND GENTLE-MEN. Quincannon stopped across the street, behind a waiting buggy drawn by a sleek dappled gray, and peered up at the lighted glass. Nothing moved behind it, at least not within the range of his vision.

He stayed where he was for a time, waiting for his head to clear completely, debating with himself. Should he talk to her again? He felt a compulsion to do so, yet he also felt that it would be futile and that it would only arouse her suspicions; he sensed that already she thought him something more than the patent medicine drummer he claimed.

He was sure she was something more than the milliner she claimed.

A single horseman trotted by, followed by a carriage with its side curtains drawn. When the carriage passed beyond where he stood he saw that the street door to the millinery shop had opened and a woman was coming out. At first he thought it was Sabina Carpenter; but then the woman picked up her skirts and hurried across the rutted street toward the buggy, and he recognized Helen Truax.

He moved out into the spillage of light from a nearby lamp. She stopped abruptly when she saw him; but after he tipped his hat and spoke to her, saying, "Good evening, Mrs. Truax," she came ahead to where he stood.

"Mr. Lyons, isn't it?"

"Yes. I hope you don't mind my speaking to you this way."

"No, it's quite all right."

Quincannon said casually, "Are you a friend of Sabina Carpenter's?"

"Why do you ask that?"

"Well, I noticed that you've just come from her shop."

"We're acquainted, yes."

Behind and above her, the second-floor window of Sabina's Millinery went dark as the lamp was extinguished. Quincannon held his gaze on it for a moment but could detect no movement behind the shadowed glass.

He said, "A new hat, then?"

"I beg your pardon?"

"The purpose of your visit tonight."

"Oh . . . yes, a new hat. If you'll excuse me, Mr. Lyons, I must be going. My husband is waiting at home."

She stepped past him to the buggy, drawing closer the white shawl she wore over her dress. In that same moment the door across the street opened again and Sabina Carpenter emerged. Quincannon still stood in the light from the street lamp; the Carpenter woman looked straight at him and he was sure she recognized him. She hesitated briefly, then pivoted and hurried away toward Washington Street.

Quincannon hesitated, too. But this was neither the time nor the place to try getting at the sense of whatever game she was playing: she would not respond well to being accosted on a dark street. And there was the matter at hand of Helen Truax. There was no telling when he might have another opportunity to speak to her alone.

Mrs. Truax was just climbing onto the tufted leather seat of the buggy. He moved over alongside as she settled herself; reached out to stroke the gray's sleek withers.

"A fine-looking horse," he said.

"Yes. My husband bought him for me."

"He must be a generous man. I spoke to him at the Paymaster this afternoon, you know."

"No, I didn't. I haven't seen him since breakfast."

"A business matter," Quincannon told her. "Concerning shares of stock in the Paymaster Mining Company."

"What shares of stock?" she asked a little sharply.

"Why, shares that might be for sale."

"To whom?"

"My employer, Mr. Arthur Caldwell of San Francisco. He is quite wealthy and his avocation is stock speculation. I often act as an unofficial scout for him. And the Paymaster would seem to be a good investment."

"Oh, I see."

"I understand you own stock in the company yourself, Mrs. Truax."

A pause. "Did my husband tell you that?"

"Yes, he did. Sabina Carpenter also remarked on it."

Another pause, longer this time; he would have liked to see her face more clearly. When she spoke again there was a tense, wary edge to her voice. "How would Miss Carpenter know about my Paymaster stock?"

"Why . . . didn't she tell you about the certificate?"

"What certificate?"

"Yours, of course — the one she found this morning. She said she intended to return it . . ."

"Well, she didn't," Helen Truax said angrily. "Where did she find it?"

"At Jason Elder's shack, she said. Perhaps she intends to return it to Mr. Elder."

"Why would she do that?"

"Well, she told me the stock belongs to him now. That you had signed it over to him."

"That's a lie!"

"You mean you do still own it?"

"Of course I own it. My husband gave it to me as a wedding present. I . . . I lost the certificate not long ago."

"Ah. I wonder what Jason Elder was doing with it?"

"I have no idea. I don't even know the man." She seemed to be making an effort to control herself. Jerkily she took up the reins. "Miss Carpenter is a liar and very likely a thief. Thank you for making me aware of the fact, Mr. Lyons. Good night."

She snapped the reins and the gray broke into a smart trot, forcing Quincannon to step back quickly from the buggy's front wheel.

He watched until Helen Truax had turned the corner on Jordan Street and passed out of sight. Then he went in the opposite direction, to Washington. There was no sign of Sabina Carpenter; he wondered if she had gone to her rooming house or if she were up to something else this night. He wondered also if the lies he had told Mrs. Truax would lead to anything revealing. A calculated risk: the time had come to stir things up a bit, even if it meant opening a hornet's nest.

He walked back to the War Eagle Hotel and took Emily Dickinson to bed.

Virginia City, Nevada.
September 9, 1892, fifty-five minutes past noon.
Hot.
He moved along the dusty backstreet on the south edge of town, toward the rear of the printing shop owned by the Stanley brothers, Ross and Adam. With him were two armed special deputies summoned by Sheriff Joseph Armitage. Armitage himself, along with two more armed deputies, was approaching from

the front. At exactly one o'clock, by their synchronized watches, the two groups would converge on the shop with weapons drawn and take the Stanley brothers into custody for the crime of counterfeiting United States Government currency.

He had arrived in Virginia City the night before, with the federal arrest warrant in his pocket. The warrant was the result of two months of investigation into a boodle game involving raised queer — greenbacks whose denomination had been increased from a low value to a high one by pasting a higher number over a lower and then overprinting a higher denomination on the face of the bill. The trail had led, circuitously, to the Stanley brothers and their printing shop, and the evidence he had gathered had been sufficient to induce a federal judge in San Francisco to issue the warrant.

This morning he had shown the warrant to Sheriff Armitage and solicited his cooperation in making the collar. The special deputies had been gathered, a plan of action worked out. And now the moment was at hand. He felt no particular tension — he had made dozens of arrests as an operative of the Secret Service — and he had seen none in the faces and actions of Armitage and the other locals. The Stanleys did not have a reputation for *courting trouble. No one anticipated any difficulty in completing the raid without incident.*

The heat on the dusty street was intense; one of the deputies mopped his streaming face with a yellow bandanna. Somewhere a dog barked, a child laughed at play. Houses lined the street, most of them run-down, their yards choked with weeds. In one yard, a makeshift swing — a barrel hoop attached to a length of rope — hung motionless from the branch of an oak tree. In another yard, clothing and bedsheets rippled in the faint, dry breeze, and the dark-haired woman who was hanging the wash turned to gaze at them curiously as they passed. He barely glanced at her; he noticed only that she was young and pregnant, her belly swollen so large that it made her clumsy when she moved.

The rear door to the printing shop was twenty yards ahead now, just beyond where the street ended at an intersecting alleyway.

He took out his stemwinder, flipped open the case. It was one minute and thirty seconds until one o'clock.

He nodded at the two deputies; all three men drew their sidearms, holding the weapons in close to their bodies. The alleyway was deserted. The only sounds, now, came from out on the street in front — the soft whinny of a horse, the rattle and squeak of a passing wagon.

They reached the alley; the rear door to the printing shop was less than ten yards away. The deputy with the yellow bandanna wiped his face again and muttered something profane about the heat.

The time was one minute before one.

And the print-shop door flew open and two men burst out at a panicked run. The Stanley brothers. The one in the lead, Ross, carried a double-barreled shotgun; the other clutched an old Army revolver.

Quincannon had not time to think; he knew by instinct that Armitage and the other deputies had stupidly let themselves be seen making their approach. He threw himself sideways into the street just as Ross Stanley, wild-eyed with terror, emptied one barrel of the shotgun. The deputy with the yellow bandanna screamed and went down. Ross jumped the pole fence into the nearest yard; his brother started to run down the alley.

The second deputy, belly-flat on the ground now, shot Adam's legs out from under him. Adam flopped around in the dust, yelling, trying to bring his revolver up for a shot; the deputy fired twice more. It was the third shot that blew away the side of Adam Stanley's head, but Quincannon didn't see that. He was already up on his feet, attempting to draw a bead on the other fugitive brother.

Ross was running sideways so that the shotgun and its remaining load were pointed in Quincannon's direction. He was almost to the fence separating that yard from the next in line, the one in which the pregnant woman still stood, frozen with shock, a white sheet stretched out in her hands like a flag of truce.

Quincannon did not see her. There was sweat in his eyes, made gritty by the dust; all he saw was Ross and the shotgun. He fired and Ross fired. The charge of buckshot exploded the top rail of the fence between them — harmlessly. Quincannon's shot missed, too. His second bullet was the one that knocked Ross over on his back and left him there unmoving, the empty shotgun canted across his bloodied chest.

The noise of the guns still echoed in Quincannon's ears; it wasn't until he got slowly and shakily to his feet that he heard the screams, rising above the shouts and running steps of Armitage and his two men. At first, confused, he thought the screams were those of the deputy who had taken the load of buckshot. But when he glanced that way he saw the man sitting up, grimacing in silence as the second deputy knelt beside him.

He looked back the other way, beyond

where Ross Stanley lay motionless in the near yard. Then he saw the woman, down on her back amid the remains of her wash, skirt pulled high on her thrashing legs, her cries lifting and falling and lifting again through the hot, dry air. And he realized with a sudden sickening anguish that his first shot hadn't been wild at all.

He dropped his weapon, ran to the fence, vaulted over it. Blood on the front of her swollen stomach, pumping through her clasped hands. Her eyes open, staring at him, accusing him. Her mouth open, the screams coming out, sliding up and down the scale, scraping at his nerve endings like a carpenter's file. Wetness blurred his vision as he fell to his knees beside her. He said something, an apology, a prayer, but she never heard him. She stopped thrashing, and her body convulsed, and he watched life pour out of her in a bright red spurt; helplessly he watched her die.

The screams went on. Long after she was dead her screams went on and on inside his head . . .

He was sitting up in bed, soaked in sweat, staring blindly into the darkness. It was a minute or more before Katherine Bennett's screams faded and he could hear the silence of the room, the distant rhythm of the stamps on War Eagle and Florida mountains.

But he could still see those eyes, accusing him; still see her life's blood and that of her unborn child pouring out between her clasped fingers. He groped the whiskey bottle off the nightstand, drank from it without bothering with a glass.

Murderer.

Murderer . . .

Chapter 10

Shortly past dawn, Quincannon roused the night hostler at Cadmon's Livery out of his bed. The liveryman rented him the same blaze-faced roan he had ridden to the Paymaster mine, and provided directions to Cow Creek and the Ox-Yoke ranch. Quincannon rode out of town to the west, on the heavily rutted wagon road to DeLamar and the Oregon border.

He sat stiff in the saddle, every now and then taking a drink from the flask in his coat pocket. The whiskey did nothing for the hangover pain in his temples and behind his eyes, but it eased the queasiness in his stomach, kept his hands steady and his thoughts dulled. The fresh bottle had cost him five dollars from the night clerk at the hotel; he would have paid fifty. He had emptied the one in his room sometime during the night.

The road followed Jordan Creek down-canyon, through Ruby City a mile below Silver and then Booneville — semi-abandoned camps whose crumbling buildings appeared to be inhabited mostly by prospectors still scouring the old, once profitable claims nearby. At Quincannon's back the sun rose and took the chill out of the early morning air. He barely noticed; the whiskey had long since made him impervious to the cold.

A mile above DeLamar he passed a pair of jerkline freighters on their way to Silver, cussing their mules the way 'skinners always did; otherwise there was no traffic on the road. DeLamar turned out to be a thriving little settlement, nestled in a cluster of little hills, its buildings strung along the sides of the canyon wherever a level place had been found to build on. Steep stairways climbed the hillsides and connected the houses, so that the whole place had the look of a white man's version of an Indian cliff-dwelling pueblo.

West of DeLamar Quincannon climbed to a ridge, and from there he could see the grass- and sage-covered sweep of the interior basin — one of the sections of rich cattle graze — and beyond that, the Oregon desert and the Parsnip Mountains. The road continued to drop, coming out of the bleak ridges and valleys of the Owyhees; the scent of sage replaced the spicy odor of juniper trees. When he reached the basin he encountered a fork: left to South Mountain, the hostler back in Silver had told him, right to Cow Creek. He swung right, into one of the little creek valleys where two or three hundred head of Herefords and Texas longhorns fatted themselves on bunchgrass. Not as many as there would have been before the disastrous winter of 1888–89, perhaps, but more than enough to sustain the ranches in the area.

Ox-Yoke was the biggest of them, he'd been told, and one of the largest in Owyhee County; he had no trouble finding it. The ranchyard contained a dozen buildings, including two bunkhouses and a separate cookshack, and a pair of corrals. Horses moved skittishly in one of the corrals; in an extension of the other, several cowhands were branding calves. The calves, separated from their mothers, were frightened and bawling, and as a result the cows penned nearby were in the same state. The commotion was what was making the horses skittish.

Quincannon dismounted near the horse corral, tied the roan, and crossed to where a big-bellied man whose stained apron identified him as the cook stood watching the branding operation. When Quincannon asked him where he might find Sudden Wheeler, the fat man jerked a thumb at the corral. "In there," he said. "You want him, you'll have to wait a spell."

"I'll wait, then. Which one is he?"

"Beanpole with the white whiskers."

The ground inside the corral had been beaten down to a fine powdery dust; through a haze of it Quincannon picked out a tall, thin old waddy with a yellow-white beard and a shock of yellow-white hair, coated now with dust, poking out from under his laloo hat. He was standing next to a sagebrush fire, sharpening a knifelike tool on a whetstone. His gray shirt and Texas leg chaps were smeared with blood.

Quincannon leaned against one of the fence rails and watched another waddy on a fast little cow pony throw a lasso loop around a calf's hind legs, jerk the animal off its feet, and then drag it to where the other hands waited. Four men fell on it, held it down and steady; a fifth, Sudden Wheeler, rapidly cut off the tip of one ear, slit and notched the dewlap under the neck, removed the horn buds on its head, and then applied a tar mixture to the wounds to prevent infection. The calf was a male; Wheeler castrated it, applied alcohol and more tar. Then the hot branding iron was lifted out of the fire and rolled against the animal's flank. A cloud of gray smoke puffed up, mingling with the powdery dust to deepen the haze inside the corral.

The dust had got into Quincannon's throat and it started him coughing. The stench of sweat, manure, burning sage, and scorched hide and hair aggravated his hangover, made his stomach churn again. He turned away from the fence, went back to where he had tied his horse, and took another drink from the flask.

He had to wait half an hour before the last of the calves had been branded and the foreman allowed the hands a rest before the next batch was shunted in. He used the time to question the fat cook and three other men who wandered into the area, but none of them could tell him much about Whistling Dixon. Wheeler was the man he wanted.

Most of the cowboys trooped to the water bucket; two others treated cuts and scratches with a milky solution made of alcohol and oil. Sudden Wheeler's left arm bore a long, bleeding scratch, but he didn't bother treating it. He drank a dipper of water, took off his laloo hat and poured a second dipper over his head to cool himself off. Away from his duties in the corral, he moved with a kind of determined slowness, as if he needed to conserve his energy; he was not a man, Quincannon thought, who would ever make a sudden move. Given the nature of cowboy humor, his nickname was inevitable.

Quincannon introduced himself as Andrew Lyons and spun the same story he had used in Silver City to explain his interest in Whistling Dixon. Wheeler seemed wary at first, but Quincannon put that down to a natural reluctance to deal with strangers in general and noncattlemen in particular. He seemed to have nothing to hide and he was not unwilling to talk once his pump had been primed.

"Sure," he said, "I knowed Whistling some. Hard man to know at all. Didn't talk to nobody. Used to josh him about his vocal chords rusting up for lack of use. No sense of humor, though; never even cracked a smile."

"When did you last see him, Mr. Wheeler?"

"My pa was Mr. Wheeler and he's been dead forty years. Call me Sudden like everybody else. Four — five weeks ago, I'd say it was. Day he quit Ox-Yoke."

"He hadn't been working here in over a month?"

"What I said."

"Why did he quit?"

Wheeler shrugged. "Close-mouthed booger, like I told you."

"Do you know where he went when he left here?"

"Up in the mountains somewheres, I reckon," Wheeler said. He had the makings out now and was rolling himself a cigarette. "Prospecting, way we all figured it. Wasn't the first time he quit to go off hunting gold. First time he done it when he was needed, though."

"Where did he do his prospecting?"

"Never talked about where. But he had him a section staked out, where he figured to make a strike. Them with the fever always do."

"It must have been somewhere near Silver City. He was seen there during the past month."

"Couple of the boys seen him, too. Don't get to Silver much myself. Don't like towns."

"Did he have any friends there that you know of?"

139

"Didn't have no friends anywhere that I know of."

"Did he ever mention a man named Jason Elder?"

"Elder? Who's he?"

"Tramp printer who worked for Will Coffin at the Owyhee *Volunteer.* He disappeared a few days ago."

"Hell. Man like Whistling wouldn't have no truck with a tramp printer."

"He knew him, though. I have proof of that."

Wheeler scratched a lucifer on his bootsole and fired his quirly. He made no comment.

Quincannon said, "People in Silver think it was outlaws who shot him. That what you think, too?"

"Must've been. Who else'd want to kill him?"

"I thought you might have some idea."

"Not me, son. Whistling was a crusty old fart, and maybe a tiny bit crooked, but he didn't have no real enemies. Never talked to nobody long enough to make himself an enemy."

"How was he a tiny bit crooked?"

"Played cards with him once. Never caught him at nothing but I wouldn't play with him again. Nobody else would, neither, that knowed him. He was allus cleaning out some young snot figured he was born to lie down with lady luck."

"Maybe he was a lot more dishonest than you thought," Quincannon said musingly.

Wheeler said nothing. That sort of speculation was something he seemed disinclined to engage in.

Quincannon asked, "Did Dixon ever mention Oliver Truax?"

"Who? Oh, fancy-pants owns the Paymaster mine. Nope. Why should he?"

"No particular reason. How about a Chinese merchant named Yum Wing?"

"Now what in holy hell would Whistling be talking about a Chinaman for? You got some funny ideas, mister. Yes you have."

"Jack Bogardus, then. Owner of the Rattling Jack mine."

"Well, now, there you got something," Wheeler said. "I recollect Whistling did mention Bogardus a time or two."

"In what way?"

"He knowed somebody works for Bogardus."

"Who?"

"Shirttail cousin of his'n, name of Conrad. Mean little booger with bad teeth and breath that'd knock a man over at twenty

141

rods. Worked here a couple of months during the spring gather."

"When did he quit?"

"Didn't quit. Boss caught him butchering one of our steers to sell to the homesteaders and threw him off Ox-Yoke land. Told him he'd be shot on sight if he ever showed his ugly face around here again."

"How did Dixon take to that?"

"Never said nothing or did nothing to tell us how he felt. Said later on Conrad went to work for Bogardus, but that's all."

"Did he say what kind of work?"

"Nope."

"What was his opinion of Bogardus? Dixon's, I mean."

"Didn't seem to have one."

"What's your opinion of him? Or don't you know him?"

"Know of him. Don't much like what I know."

"Crooked?"

"Like a dog's hind leg, some say."

"How so? Anything specific?"

"None I heard about."

"Any of the other hands who might have an idea?"

"Doubtful. I'd of heard the idea if there was." Wheeler took a last drag on his cigarette and pitched the butt away. But his

142

bright old eyes remained on Quincannon's face. "You ask a heap of questions for a drummer, Mr. Lyons," he said at length.

"A natural inquisitiveness," Quincannon said.

"You figure maybe Whistling wasn't killed by outlaws? That maybe Bogardus done it?"

"I don't know, Sudden. That's why I'm asking questions."

"Marshal's job, ain't it?"

"He's only one man. A lawman in country like this can always use help."

"No argument there," Wheeler said. He shrugged. "None of my business anyways, I reckon. My business is cows."

He turned as he spoke: another group of hands had arrived with more wet stock and was driving the cows and calves into the pens. The foreman began calling for the branding team, raising his voice to a shout to make himself heard above the terrified bawling of the animals.

Wheeler said, "Work to be done. Hope you get what you're after, son."

"So do I."

Quincannon watched the old waddy climb back inside the corral and cross to the sagebrush fire. Then he moved off to where the new hands were dismounting

143

near the barn. None of them could tell him any more than Sudden Wheeler had, except that Dixon's shirttail cousin, Conrad, was good with a handgun and "a mean little son of a bitch drunk or sober."

It was past noon when Quincannon rode out of Ox-Yoke. His hangover had faded some at the ranch, but after half an hour in the saddle, under the full glare of the sun, it began to plague him again. The morning's whiskey and the growling emptiness in his belly made him dizzy. He cursed himself for not buying some beefsteak and sourdough biscuits from the Ox-Yoke cook.

When he reached DeLamar he stopped at the first cafe he saw and forced down a plate of beans and bacon. Afterward he went to a nearby saloon and drank two pints of Gretes' beer, the home brew, to slake his thirst. He felt better then. Well enough, at least, to face the steady, up-canyon climb to Silver City.

A mile below Ruby City he had to stop and wait while two wagons maneuvered around each other on a ledge where the road narrowed and there was a sheer dropoff on one side. On impulse he asked one of the drivers, who had paused after the passage to check a wheel hub, if he knew where the Rattling Jack mine was located. The man said he did and gave directions. The route would take Quincannon south away from Silver, toward the Ruby Mountains, but the distance was not great. It would mean another half hour of riding, no more. He had enough whiskey left for that.

Between Ruby and Silver, a narrow and badly rutted wagon road cut away to the south and he turned along there. It snaked through a network of hollows and swells, forked twice — he took the left fork each time, as per the wagon driver's instructions — and finally climbed along a bare shoulder on the south side of War Eagle Mountain. The sun was westering now and the high-plateau wind had picked up; it blew cool against his face, bent the sage and bunchgrass on the slope and made whistling noises among the rocks.

He heard the dull thud of the Rattling Jack's small stamp mill before he saw any sign of the mine. He put the roan into a slow walk as they started around a sharp turning in the road. Then the mine's surface works appeared, sitting forward on the slope beyond the ravine he had been skirting, and he drew rein. Black-painted words on the side of the largest of the mine buildings spelled out the words: RATTLING JACK MINING CO.

Two things about the place struck him immediately as odd. One was the fence that enclosed the compound — a tall, horseshoe-shaped stockade fence, the kind that might have been erected in the days when roving bands of Bannacks and Piutes attacked isolated diggings; now it seemed an excessive precaution, unless Bogardus were hiding something behind it. The second thing was the tailings. The biggest drift of them looked old, evidence of what had once been a large-scale operation here. There was a newer dump, below a tramway that extended out over the stockade fence, but it was small — too small for a mine where a rich new vein had been found and worked for some months. Truax had said Bogardus claimed to be producing ore that assayed at a hundred dollars a ton, which was impossible with a dump that size.

Quincannon dismounted, led the roan back around the turning, ground-reined it, and then made his way up along the side of the slope to its highest vantage point, where he could just see over the top of the fence. But the distance was considerable; he wished he had rented a spyglass along with the horse. He studied as much of the compound as he could see. Its fourth side was a steep, almost vertical bluff. Scaleable? He would have to go up on its rim to determine that. Smoke and steam came from the roof stacks of the main shaft house and the mill at the foot of the grade, and the stamps continued their rhythmic pounding. If there was any above-ground activity, he couldn't see any of it from here. But no one trundled an ore cart out along the tram, to dump waste rock from its end — not once in the fifteen minutes Quincannon sat watching.

Nothing else happened during those fifteen minutes. Finally he stood and went back downslope to his horse. Mounting, he headed back toward the main road and Silver City.

Something curious was going on at the Rattling Jack; he was convinced of that now. But it was premature to assume that Bogardus and his men were the koniakers. More information was needed before he could make that assumption and take action on it.

Still, what better place for the manufacture of bogus coins and notes than an isolated silver mine?

Chapter 11

The hands on Quincannon's stemwinder showed a quarter of five when he rode into downtown Silver. He tied up in front of the Wells Fargo office and went in to ask the Western Union telegrapher if a wire had come for him. None had; Boggs was taking longer than he had hoped to reply to his request for information, doubtless because that information was not easy to come by.

He rode down to Cadmon's Livery, turned over the roan to the day hostler, Henry, and walked to the War Eagle Hotel. There, he found a message waiting — from Sabina Carpenter, asking him to call on her either at her millinery shop or at Mrs. Farnsworth's rooming house on Morning Star Street. He was not surprised. Nor was he reluctant to see her; the prospect gave him an odd sense of anticipation.

Upstairs in his room, he washed the trail dust out of his beard and off his skin and brushed it from his clothing. He held his hands up when he was done, watched them for a moment. Steady. But he took a drink anyway, a large one, before he went downstairs again.

It was not yet six o'clock, so he went first to Avalanche Avenue. The street door to Sabina's Millinery was unlocked. He entered and climbed a flight of stairs that delivered him into a spacious single room with draperies drawn across the rear third of it to create a private compartment. There was no one in the public two thirds of the room.

He paused for a moment to take stock of the place. A display table with four finished hats — two for men, two for women — arranged on little stands. Another, much larger table on which were a bolt of cloth, scissors, and a tape measure. Shelves containing more bolts in a variety of colors and patterns. Other shelves stacked with artificial flowers, grosgrain and velvet ribbons, black and white veil netting, boxes of hatpins, different kinds of bows and doodads. The shop struck him, unlike the Rattling Jack mine, as a legitimate business operation. He wondered if Sabina Carpenter had purchased the existing stock from a former owner or if she had brought it all with her from Denver or wherever she'd come.

"Miss Carpenter?"

The draperies parted and she appeared. Today she wore a dark blue shirtwaist and a striped serge skirt; her dark hair was piled high on her head and fastened with a lacquered comb — a style that gave her a vaguely Oriental appearance and made almost nonexistent her resemblance to Katherine Bennett. She did not smile as she came toward him, nor did she offer her hand. The look in her eyes was unreadable.

"Thank you for coming," she said in a flat voice.

"Not at all. My pleasure."

"Is it? I thought you might be unwilling to face me."

"Why should I be unwilling?"

"Because of the lies you have been telling about me."

He feigned surprise. "Lies? I don't know what you mean."

"Another lie, Mr. Lyons. If that *is* your name."

"Do you think it might not be?"

"I have my suspicions. About your profession, too."

"And why is that?"

150

"Patent medicine drummers don't usually spread falsehoods about people they scarcely know," she said. "Nor do they ask the sort of questions you have been asking around town."

"How could you know what sort of questions I've been asking?"

"I have ears," she said. "I've heard them repeated."

"Indeed? You seem to have considerable interest in me. I don't suppose it's personal?"

"Not in the sense you mean."

"Then why should a simple milliner find me so intriguing?"

"Do you think I'm not a simple milliner?"

"I, too, have my suspicions."

They looked at each other in silence for several seconds. Quincannon felt a stirring that was undeniably sexual — the first such carnal desire he had had since that day in Nevada last summer. It repelled him, because of her resemblance to Katherine Bennett, and yet the more he fought it in his mind, the stronger it became.

Sabina Carpenter seemed somehow to sense the direction of his thoughts. A faint flush colored her cheeks; abruptly she turned away, went to the Argand lamp on one wall. Twilight was approaching and shadows had begun to lengthen in the room. She lit the lamp, turned up the wick to crowd the shadows back into the corners.

When she turned to face him again she remained standing where she was. She said, "Why did you lie to Helen Truax last night? Why did you say I'd told you about finding her shares of Paymaster stock?"

He shrugged. "I merely stretched the truth a little. Mrs. Truax seemed eager for the stock certificate to be returned to her."

She made no response.

Quincannon said, "Ah," and smiled faintly.

"That stock certificate is none of your concern."

"Perhaps not. Unless it pertains to the death of my old friend Whistling Dixon."

She was not prepared for that. The statement seemed to puzzle and confuse her for a moment. Finally she said, "I fail to understand how the murder of a cowboy could be connected to Helen Truax and the Paymaster Mining Company."

"You found the certificate in Jason Elder's shack, with her shares signed over to him. And Elder was acquainted with Whistling Dixon — well enough acquainted so that Dixon was carrying Elder's watch when he was shot."

Confusion showed in her face again. She seemed about to speak, then held her tongue.

"Mrs. Truax denies having signed the stock over to anyone," he said. "Now why do you suppose *she* lied?"

"I'm sure I have no idea."

"Nor any idea why she should give what amounts to twelve thousand dollars to a tramp printer addicted to opium?"

"No."

"What happened to Jason Elder, Miss Carpenter?"

"Happened to him? What makes you think something happened to him?"

"It's rather obvious, isn't it?"

"Not to me."

"Oh yes, that's right," Quincannon said. "You scarcely knew the man; you were only making a new hat for him . . . a fancy new hat for a man who lived in a shack and preferred to spend his money on opium."

The corners of her mouth tightened into white ridges; she was angry now. It was plain that she did not like to be put on the defensive. "I find your insinuations objectionable and irritating," she said. "Particularly so since you are a liar and no doubt

153

worse — for all I know, a common criminal, even a murderer."

Murderer, he thought, and Katherine Bennett began thrashing in his mind again, the blood pumping out between her clasped hands, the accusing eyes boring into his. He heard her screams again and he watched her die again.

Sabina Carpenter said, "Why are you so interested in Whistling Dixon's death and Jason Elder's disappearance?"

"I told you why. Dixon was like a second father to me when I was a boy."

"I don't believe that. And I don't believe you're interested in the Truaxes and the Paymaster Mining Company because of Dixon's death, either. Just who are you, Mr. Lyons?"

"A salesman for a brand of salts," Quincannon said. "Just as you are a maker of hats for ladies and gentlemen and tramp printers."

She hesitated, then moved to within two paces of him. Flushed with her anger, her face had a radiant quality in the lampglow and the fading daylight; he stared hard at it, to keep from staring at a face inside his mind. Her eyes were a dark brown, he saw, almost black in this light. Her mouth was full, the lips soft-looking. There was a sprinkling of tiny freckles across the bridge of her nose.

She said, "Answer me this, then. What do you intend to do next?"

"When I leave here, you mean?"

"You know what I mean. About Helen Truax, for one. Do you intend to see her again?"

"Perhaps."

"To discuss her relationship with Jason Elder?"

"Perhaps."

"Do you intend to tell her husband about Elder? About the stock certificate?"

"Would you rather I didn't?"

"It wouldn't be prudent or scrupulous."

"Neither was your keeping the certificate after you found it. Or did you turn it over to Marshal McClew after all?"

She was silent.

Quincannon said, "Oliver Truax does have a right to know about his wife's indiscretions, whatever they may be. With Elder, and with Jack Bogardus, too."

"Bogardus? What do you know about Mrs. Truax's relationship with him?"

"I might ask you the same thing. What do *you* know about their relationship?"

No answer.

"Well then," he said, "what do you know

about the Rattling Jack mine?"

She frowned, showing puzzlement again. "The Rattling Jack has nothing to do with Mrs. Truax."

"Perhaps not. But she *is* involved with Bogardus, isn't she?"

"I have no intention of trading gossip with you, Mr. Lyons. Helen Truax's personal life is her own concern; her privacy ought to be respected. Passing on rumors and idle speculation to her husband can do no one any good."

"Including you?"

"And what does that imply?"

"You're familiar with the word blackmail, aren't you, Miss Carpenter?"

She glared at him. "How dare you," she said.

It was his turn not to respond. A silence settled between them, heavy and tense; they stood with their gazes locked. Her eyes had little flecks of light in them, like mica particles reflecting the sun. The tip of her tongue made a wet line between her pursed lips. He could hear the faint rasp of her breathing. He could smell the delicate scent of her lilac perfume.

He kissed her.

It was the most impetuous thing he had ever done in his life. It surprised him even more than it surprised her, because he had had no thought of doing it; it was just something he found himself doing, and afterward couldn't explain even to himself.

She didn't fight him, but neither did she respond. She endured the moment, and when he released her and stepped back, she slapped him. A ringing slap, with enough strength behind it to rock him and leave his cheek burning under its mat of beard.

"When I want to be kissed," she said in a low, wintry voice, "I offer an invitation. And I prefer to invite a man who doesn't reek of whiskey."

Self-disgust moved through him. He felt suddenly bewildered, wretched, a wriggling thing that had crawled out from under a rock and assaulted her.

Murderer. Murderer.

Not meeting her gaze now, he said, "I apologize, Miss Carpenter. Vulgar and inexcusable of me." The words had an abject sound in his ears, almost sniveling.

"I think you should leave," she said.

"Yes. I . . . yes."

He went to the stairs, hurried down them without looking back at her. Outside, he stood for a moment in the cold sweep of the wind, letting it take the heat out of his

Chapter 12

He went south on Jordan, into Silver's red light district near Long Gulch Creek, and found his way into a deadfall called Mother Mack's. The place was bedlam — two pianos competing with each other, hurdy-gurdy girls dancing with burly miners and leaned-down cowpunchers, roulette and faro and chuck-a-luck games receiving heavy play, and a noisy poker match in progress in one corner. Quincannon found elbow room at the bar and drank two double whiskeys in rapid succession. This was the place for him tonight, the kind of low dive he belonged in. The haunt of whores, sure-thing men, bunco steerers, thieves — and other murderers. They were fitting company for the likes of him.

He ordered a third whiskey, and would have drunk it straightaway, to obliterate Katherine Bennett and Sabina Carpenter from his thoughts, if the man next to him hadn't departed just then and left a copy of the Owyhee *Volunteer* on the bar.

It was the most recent edition, the one that had come out this day, and Quincannon saw that it carried a front-page editorial under the heading ANOTHER CHINESE OUTRAGE. He drew the paper over in front of him. Will Coffin had waxed eloquent and indignant over the second illegal entry of the newspaper office, accusing "unsavory elements of the Chinese population, among them the scurvy merchant Yum Wing" as the culprits and claiming that the crimes were "in retaliation for public condemnation, in this newspaper, of the vicious practices of selling opium and encouraging opium addiction in our fair city." He went on to say that "anyone guilty of such mean acts, whether he be a Chinaman or a white man, would steal the leather hinges off a blind woman's smokehouse and ought to be dealt with accordingly. The time has come to put an end to such open lawlessness, a fact with which City Marshal Wendell McClew must surely agree."

Quincannon pushed the paper aside. Chinaman or white man, he thought.

He drank his third whiskey, slowly. His mind seemed clear again, empty for the moment of the self-loathing that had brought him here, focused once more on the business at hand. One of the hurdy-gurdy girls began to rub her bosom against his arm, to murmur enticements — half an hour of dancing for fifty cents, more intimate activities for a dollar and up. Her voice and her painted face repelled him; he brushed her away. The deadfall itself repelled him now: he no more belonged in this part of society than he did among the cloistered rich on San Francisco's Nob Hill. He belonged to no part of society, not anymore. He was a man alone, who answered to no one on this earth, not even the United States Government; who would answer only to God.

He threaded a path through the noisy throng, went outside, and put Mother Mack's behind him. For the first block he was a little unsteady on his feet, but the wind soon remedied that. He walked up Washington Street and over to the office of the *Volunteer*, found it dark. From the third passerby he stopped he learned that Will Coffin's home was on Union Street, off Morning Star north of Jordan Creek.

He found his way to Union Street. Coffin's house was a weathered frame structure perched apart from others on the steep hillside, with a second-story privy curiously set on stilts and connected to the house by a catwalk. Lamplight made a yellow rectangle of the front window. He climbed the stairs, lifted the brass knocker on the door, and let it fall.

It took Coffin almost a minute to respond. He was in shirtsleeves and stocking feet, galluses down and his hemp-colored hair tousled; he blinked sleepily at Quincannon, stifled a yawn, and said, "Well, you do surprise me, Mr. Lyons. This is the second unexpected visit from you in two days."

"Have I come at a bad time, Mr. Coffin?"

"No, no. I was reading and I must have fallen asleep. I was up until all hours last night, getting out this week's edition of the paper."

"Yes, I've just seen it. An impressive editorial."

"Thank you. I rather thought so myself."

"The editorial is the reason I've come tonight. Can we talk inside? It's a bit chilly out here."

"Of course."

Coffin led the way into the front sitting room. "I can offer you a brandy, if you like. I don't keep whiskey on hand, I'm afraid."

Quincannon hesitated, but then shook his head. "Thank you, no. I expect I won't be staying long."

"Well then. Sit down and tell me what's on your mind."

Coffin moved a heavy volume of Shakespeare off a Morris chair and settled himself down in its place; Quincannon sat on an overstuffed divan. A wood fire burned in the grate nearby. Its warmth took away the night's chill that had lingered on his face and hands.

He said, "I'm curious about the illegal entries into the newspaper office and your home. Just how many were there altogether?"

"Two at the office and one here."

"Was anything stolen on those three occasions?"

"Not that I have been able to determine."

"Was there any vandalizing done?"

"Not of the usual sort, no. Files, type, clothing and such were strewn around, but nothing was deliberately destroyed."

Quincannon said, "That sounds as if the culprits might have been searching for something."

"Searching?" Coffin frowned. "What the devil could those heathens have been searching for at the *Volunteer* office or among my personal effects?"

"You're certain it *was* the Chinese who were responsible?"

"Of course I am."

"Then you found evidence that pointed to one or more of their number?"

"No," Coffin admitted, "no physical evidence. But the first break-in occurred the evening my first anti-opium editorial appeared in the *Volunteer*. I've angered no white man in Silver, made no other enemies. It could be no one *but* the Chinamen."

"I see," Quincannon said, and what he saw was the bigoted inflexibility of Coffin's perceptions. He mused for a time. Then he said, "Tell me, did Jason Elder happen to give you anything for safekeeping before he disappeared?"

The question made the newspaperman frown again. "No, he did not. What are you implying? That the Chinamen invaded my office and home looking for something that belongs to Elder? That is preposterous."

"Perhaps it wasn't the Chinese who broke in after all," Quincannon said.

"White men? I still say the notion is preposterous. What could Elder own of sufficient value to warrant three illegal entries?"

What, indeed? Quincannon thought. He made no reply.

Coffin said, "Your interest in Jason Elder strikes me as excessive. Do you believe he had something to do with the death of your friend Whistling Dixon?"

"It is possible, isn't it?"

"Not to my mind. Elder disappeared some time before Dixon was shot."

"From public view, yes. Not necessarily from the Owyhees. And the two of them *were* acquainted."

"You've found that out, have you?" Coffin gave him a long, calculating look. "You know, you're rather a persistent and inquisitive fellow for a drummer. You act more like a lawman — a detective I once knew in Kansas City."

Quincannon laughed. "Hardly that, Mr. Coffin. My tolerance for violence is much too low and my fondness for whiskey much too high."

The answer had its desired effect: Coffin laughed, too, and seemed to dismiss the notion, at least for the time being. He said, "Well, you do seem overly concerned about Dixon's death — a man you hadn't seen in a good many years."

"Whistling Dixon and I were very close

when I was a youngster," Quincannon said, making his voice and his manner intense. "His murder . . . well, it was quite a shock, happening as it did the very night I arrived in Silver City. I find myself just a bit obsessed with identifying the man or men who killed him. You can understand how I feel, I'm sure."

"I suppose I can."

"I haven't spoken to Marshal McClew. Has he uncovered any leads of his own, do you know?"

"He hasn't," Coffin said. "I had a drink with him not two hours ago."

"How did he feel about your editorial?"

A wry smile. "He didn't like it. He is of the opinion that I'm trying to foment racial strife, which is ridiculous. He thinks the damned heathens are a peace-loving bunch and ought to be left alone."

Quincannon's estimate of the marshal rose a notch; McClew might after all be a man whose confidence he would want to enter into. He said, "Then the marshal doesn't share your certainty of their guilt?"

"He says he has no proof either way. He even refuses to interrogate Yum Wing, much less close down his filthy opium-peddling operation. I am beginning to believe that Oliver Truax is right: vigilante action is the only sure course of action open to us."

"Violence is seldom the answer to any problem, Mr. Coffin."

"Are you a pacifist? Not that it matters. I have no intention of debating the matter with you. You are not the victim of Oriental harassment and I am."

There was no arguing with the man; Coffin's prejudice acted on his judgment as a pair of blinders acted on a horse's vision, making it impossible for him to take any but the narrowest view. Quincannon said, "As you wish, then," and got to his feet. "I'll be leaving now. With thanks for your time and hospitality."

Coffin made a dismissive gesture. "I'll show you out." At the door he said, "I wish you success in your quest, Mr. Lyons. Nothing would please me more than to write a story for the *Volunteer* about justice served."

"Justice usually is served," Quincannon said, "in one way or another." He started out onto the porch and then paused. "Before I go, would you happen to know a man named Conrad who works for Jack Bogardus at the Rattling Jack mine? He's a shirttail cousin of Whistling Dixon's, I've learned."

"Conrad? No, I can't say I do."

"You do know Bogardus, though?"

"I know him," Coffin said with distaste. "A ruffian and a fornicator."

"But a successful miner for all of that. Oliver Truax told me the Rattling Jack's new vein assays at one hundred dollars a ton."

"I suspect that sum is a gross exaggeration. Bogardus certainly doesn't freight out much silver."

"He doesn't?"

"No. The man who runs the Poison Creek station is a personal friend of mine. He has told me that he seldom sees Bogardus' wagons on the Boise or Nampa roads."

Quincannon took his leave. As he started downhill to Morning Star Street, he considered what he had learned from Coffin. The information about Bogardus and the Rattling Jack coincided with his suspicions. It also tended to eliminate the possibility of a link between Coffin and Bogardus; if Bogardus *was* the leader of the koniakers, it seemed unlikely that Coffin, in view of the man's candor, was the engraver of the plates for the counterfeit notes. Jason Elder was still the most probable candidate.

But what happened to Elder? And what,

if Quincannon's hunch was correct, could he have possessed that had prompted a ransacking of his shack and the illegal entry of the newspaper office and Coffin's home? Helen Truax's shares of stock in the Paymaster Mining Company were one possibility; the searchers had evidently overlooked the certificate at Elder's shack. Yet the stock seemed a minor prize, hardly worth the effort and risk of *three* separate break-ins. It seemed important only to Helen Truax, her husband, and Jason Elder himself.

Whatever the object of the hunt, what had Elder done with it? The man had no friends in Silver City. He hadn't given it to his employer. And assume for the moment that he hadn't hidden it where he lived. Was there anyone else to whom he might have entrusted such a valued object?

Yum Wing.

Quincannon cursed himself for being slow-witted, too befuddled by whiskey to see the obvious truth of the matter long before this. Elder was or had been an opium addict; who better to take into his trust than the man who supplied him with his daily ticket to the land of celestial dreams. And Yum Wing had plainly been hiding something behind his Oriental stoicism yesterday: His refusal to discuss Elder proved that.

At Jordan Street, Quincannon turned uphill toward the Chinese colony. Not surprisingly, considering the hour, he found Yum Wing's store closed and dark. Across the street and a dozen yards farther uphill, excited Chinese voices and the click of Mah-Jongg tiles came from inside the meeting hall. He considered going there to ask where Yum Wing lived, but he had spent enough time among the Chinese to know that he would not be welcome in such a place and that his questions might not be answered. Instead, he turned along the uphill side of the store, thinking that he might find a way inside at the rear. He was not above nocturnal breaking-and-entering himself, if it might serve a useful purpose.

The darkness was thick and clotted back there, forcing him to move slowly. But when he came to the rear corner, starshine and the pale wedge of a moon let him see that there was a second building tucked in behind a knobby outcrop. It was connected to the store by a long, narrow shed that would probably serve as a covered passageway between the two and keep Yum Wing dry during the heavy winter snows. Because of the outcrop, neither the second dwelling nor the shed could be seen from downhill on Jordan Street.

Quincannon moved along parallel to the shed, out away from it to avoid the heaviest shadows that crouched there. There was light inside the house; he could make out the glow against the darkness around back, where the outside door must be. The near side wall was empty of windows or doors. He turned the corner. One window in that wall, but it was curtained in monk's cloth; the light came through the partially open door beyond. He took a step toward the door, putting his hand on the Remington holstered inside his coat.

Something moved in the shadows behind him.

He heard the sound, knew it as the scraping of a boot-sole, and came around swiftly, drawing his weapon as he did. But still he was not quick enough. There were two of them, blobs of black rushing toward him from the side wall; the smaller one hit him first, a glancing blow over his right eye. He grunted and staggered sideways with the stench of the man's rancid breath in his nostrils. The second one slashed him across the side of the neck with what must have been a gun barrel. He went to his knees, his senses jarred awry. Tried to get up and couldn't find the strength.

The smaller man kicked him in the side, toppling and rolling him, then kicked him twice more and drove him up against the building wall. The pain brought a groaning sound out of his throat. Distantly, through the blood pulsing in his ears, he could hear the two of them talking in low, urgent whispers.

"That's enough. We make any more noise, some of the other Chinamen might hear."

"Hell with them yella-skinned bastards." Another vicious kick, in the stomach this time, that brought up the whiskey Quincannon had drunk earlier.

"That's enough, I said! We got what we come for. You want to be seen now, for Christ's sake?"

Shuffling noises on the hard-packed earth. A muttered epithet. And then the sounds of them moving away, sounds that faded and were lost in the humming and buzzing in his ears.

He lay there hurting, only half conscious, for a space of time. Then he was on his knees, vomiting. Then he was groping his way up the rough clapboards, leaning against them and holding on for fear his shaking legs would give way under him.

Something wet, blood or sweat, flowed down over one cheek and dripped off the end of his chin. He didn't bother to wipe it off — just stood there shivering in the cold wind. It was another minute or two before the pulsing inside his head went away and his thoughts settled and he was able to think rationally again.

We got what we come for.

Quincannon pushed away from the wall, stumbled but held his balance. He touched the holster under his coat, found it empty, and simply recalled the revolver being knocked from his hand; it was somewhere on the ground, hidden now in the darkness. Find it later, he thought, and moved back around the corner, toward the open door to Yum Wing's quarters.

Inside, on a black-lacquered chest, an Aladdin lamp bathed the room in a dusky yellow glow. It let him see Yum Wing almost immediately. They had hung him from a support beam in one corner, at an outward angle so that his sandal-shod feet seemed braced against the wall. The expression on his dead face was ghastly in the pale light.

The rest of the room was a shambles; Yum Wing had put up a fight before he died. *We got what we come for.* The smell of death was strong in there, but it was another smell that Quincannon was remembering as he backed out of the room — the rancid stench of the small man's breath.

Sudden Wheeler's voice echoed across his mind: *mean little booger with bad teeth and breath that'd knock a man over at twenty rods.*

Conrad, Whistling Dixon's shirttail cousin.

Conrad, who now worked for Jack Bogardus at the Rattling Jack mine.

Chapter 13

When Quincannon came downstairs at nine the next morning he found a message waiting at the hotel desk. Marshal Wendell McClew had sent word that he wanted to see Andrew Lyons in his office "any time before noon."

He considered the request as he left the hotel. He doubted that it had anything to do with the murder of Yum Wing; he was reasonably certain that he hadn't been seen leaving the Chinese quarter last night. If he was under suspicion for that or any other crime, McClew would not have sent a message; he would have come in person and either talked in Quincannon's room or put him in custody. No, it was probably that McClew had heard about the questions he'd been asking, from Will Coffin perhaps, and wanted a first-hand explanation.

Quincannon walked up Jordan Street,

moving at a retarded pace. His ribs ached and there were stabs of pain whenever he took any but shallow breaths. None of the ribs was broken or cracked, but half a dozen on his right side were badly bruised. Except for his slow movements, and a cut above one temple that he had treated with carbolic salve, he bore no outward signs of the beating he had taken at Yum Wing's. But inside he carried a bitter rage that was thinly contained.

He reached the Wells Fargo office, entered to talk to the Western Union brass pounder. And finally found a wire waiting from Boggs. It was more fully coded than his own had been, for obvious reasons, but the telegrapher seemed to think nothing of it. Such codes were common among businessmen who preferred that their long-distance dealings remain private.

BUSINESS SLOW HERE STOP GLAD TO LEARN OF FRUITFUL POSSIBILITIES YOUR TERRITORY DESPITE BANKRUPT ACCOUNT STOP GREENSPAN ENROUTE BOISE WILL JOIN YOU ASAP STOP WMC RECORD GOOD FORMER CAP OR VOL TWICE DEC BRAV STOP MY REGARDS HT AND JB BOTH PORTLAND STOP FORMER SAL

HOS LATTER MIN LAB AG AMONG
OTHERS STOP SHARED ADDRESS
AND BADGER FOUR YEARS AGO NO
CON STOP PARTED AFTER DISPUTE
NOTHING THEREAFTER STOP RECON-
CILIATION QMK REGARDING OT
HINT PMC POSSIBLE FMFM BUT NO
CORROBORATION YET STOP STILL
CHECKING OTHER MATTERS

ARTHUR CALDWELL

Quincannon folded the wire and tucked
it into his coat pocket. The news that his
fellow Service operative, Samuel Greenspan, was on his way from Seattle to Silver
City was reassuring; matters here appeared
to be escalating to the point where he
would need as many allies as possible. It
appeared that Marshal Wendell McClew
might well be another one. The fact that
McClew had a good record as a peace officer, and the added facts that he was a
former captain with the Oregon Volunteers
during the War Between the States, and
had been twice decorated for bravery, testi-
fied in favor of his competency and his
honesty.

The rest of Boggs' information was eye-opening, and answered some of the questions that had arisen the past few days. Helen Truax and Jack Bogardus were both from Portland, where she had worked as a saloon hostess and he had been a mining labor agitator, among other dubious undertakings; and they had not only known each other there but had lived together four years ago. "Shared badger no con" meant that they had worked a version of the old badger game, in which an amorous married man's indiscretion was used as grounds for blackmail, and had managed to escape criminal conviction. This put a new light on Helen Truax's character. If Bogardus *was* one of the koniakers, as seemed more and more likely, and Mrs. Truax had taken up with him again here in Silver City, then it was conceivable that she, too, was involved in the boodle game.

The telegram suggested that there might also be another game afoot here, one in which Helen Truax could also be involved. "Regarding OT hint PMC possible fmfm" meant that Oliver Truax was apparently responsible for some sort of illegal manipulation or flimflam involving Paymaster Mining Company stock. Boggs hadn't yet been able to find out what it was. If the allegation were true it explained Truax's eagerness to sell Paymaster stock to the mythical Arthur Caldwell of San Francisco.

Was there a connection between the counterfeiting operation and the Paymaster flimflam? It seemed unlikely, considering the obvious hatred Truax and Jack Bogardus shared for each other. Yet Helen Truax was the wife of one man and the mistress, past and present, of the other. . . .

Quincannon wanted another talk with her. And another talk with her husband. But both could wait until after he had responded to Marshal McClew's summons, something he did not want to put off. Besides, there was a chance Boggs would wire him again today, and the more he knew, the easier it would be to deal with both of the Truaxes.

He sent a telegram to San Francisco, laboring over it to give Boggs the full measure of his suspicions about Bogardus and the Rattling Jack mine without sacrificing secrecy. He also asked that as many other federal officers as were available be sent to Boise on a standby basis. He had to have more proof against Bogardus before he would be justified in calling for a federal arrest warrant and then organizing a raid on the Raffling Jack. The time when he would have sufficient justification, he felt, was not far off.

Leaving the Wells Fargo office, he went to a nearby saloon for a brace of whiskeys and a pickled egg. There was talk in the place of Yum Wing's murder; the body had been found by other Chinese early this morning and word brought to the marshal's office. No one seemed particularly stirred by the news. "Don't make no difference who killed him," the bartender said. "Did the community a service. Like it said in yesterday's paper, opium's filthy stuff; man who sells it ain't no better than a dog."

Quincannon left the bartender to his bias and walked over to Washington Street to the courthouse. The marshal's office was in the basement; he passed under the sign that said JAIL, went down three steps and through a heavy ironbound door. McClew was the only occupant, seated at a battered kneehole desk with a mug of coffee and a plate of eggs and potatoes in front of him. Egg yolk stained his mustaches; a splatter of it had even somehow found its way onto the brim of his plug hat. He looked up as Quincannon entered, gestured with his fork toward a slat-backed chair near the desk, and went on eating.

Quincannon sat down. Somebody behind a closed door that would lead to the cellblock began yelling in a hoarse voice, "Marshal! Hey, Marshal! Goddamn it, where's my goddamn breakfast? You promised me my goddamn breakfast two hours ago!"

McClew lifted his head and yelled over his shoulder, "Shut up. Dewey, or I'll come in there and knock your goddamn head off your goddamn shoulders." Dewey subsided. McClew nodded, said to Quincannon, "Drunks is bad enough when they're drunk but they're worse pains in the arse the morning after," and forked a last bite of egg into his mouth. Then he finished his coffee, belched, used his tie to wipe the egg yolk off his mustaches (but not off his plug hat), and sat back comfortably with his hands folded over his middle.

"I am Andrew Lyons, Marshal," Quincannon said.

"I gathered." McClew studied him for a time. "Looks like you had yourself some trouble, son."

"Trouble?"

"That cut on your head. And you move kind of stiff, like a man that's been in a fight."

181

Quincannon laughed. "I have a touch of lumbago. As for the cut . . . well, I hesitate to admit it, but I'm a bit clumsy. I tripped over the throw rug in my room last night and struck my head against the bedpost."

"Uh-huh," McClew said noncommittally. He gestured at a crusty old pot-bellied stove in one corner. "Coffee's hot, if you're interested."

"Thanks, no. What was it you wanted to see me about, Marshal?"

"Questions," McClew said.

"Sir?"

"Questions. The ones you been asking all over town."

"About Whistling Dixon, you mean?"

"Among other folks. Awful lot of questions for a snake oil drummer, seems like."

"I am not a snake oil drummer," Quincannon said in offended tones. "I am an authorized representative of Caldwell Associates of San Francisco, agents for Dr. Wallmann's Nerve and Brain Salts — a legitimate and highly respected patent medicine."

McClew shrugged. "Still and all, you ask a lot of questions for *any* kind of drummer."

"Whistling Dixon was a friend from many years ago. He worked for my father in Oregon when I was a boy."

"Is that a fact?"

"Yes. Naturally I was upset when I learned he'd been murdered the very night I arrived in Silver City."

"Naturally. So you figured you'd just ask around and see could you find out who done for him."

"Yes."

"How come you asked half the town but you never come and asked me? Seems the city marshal's office'd be your first stop."

"I tried several times to see you, Marshal," Quincannon lied. "Our paths never seemed to cross."

"Oh, come on now, Mr. Lyons," McClew said mildly. "I ain't all that hard to find. Most of the time I'm right here in my office."

"Most of the time, perhaps. Not all the time. I'm sorry, but I did intend to talk to you. I would have come here this morning, in fact, even if you hadn't summoned me."

"Well, I sure am happy to hear that," McClew said without irony. He rummaged a plug of Rock Candy chewing tobacco out of his vest pocket, sliced off a chunk with a penknife, and popped the chunk into his mouth. He chewed in silence for several seconds, working the quid to a juiciness;

then he leaned over, spat into a dented brass cuspidor, and said, "Nothing like a good chew after breakfast."

"I prefer a pipe myself."

"Pipes is all right, I guess." The marshal spat again. "Tell me, Mr. Lyons, you find out anything about old Dixon's murder I ought to know about?"

"No, nothing. I've been wasting my time, it seems."

"Well, you must've found out *something*. You been seeing a lot of folks, asking about others besides Dixon. Jason Elder, for instance."

"Elder was an acquaintance of Dixon's and he seems to have disappeared. I thought perhaps there might be some connection between the two facts."

"Such as maybe Elder shot that old waddy?"

"Such as that."

"Where'd you hear them two was acquainted?"

"Here and there. I don't remember exactly."

"Never knew old Dixon to have any friends in town, least of all a tramp printer that smoked opium for a hobby."

Quincannon spread his hands. "I only know what I heard. You don't believe Elder

184

might have murdered Dixon?"

"Nope."

"Then who do you think *did* kill him?"

"Can't say. Outlaws, maybe."

"So then you haven't learned anything definite, either."

"Maybe I have and maybe I haven't," McClew said evasively. "I'm working on it."

"I'm sure you are."

"Yep, always working, that's me. I'm a working fool. Too much crime these days — too damned much."

Quincannon was silent.

"You take murder, now," McClew said. "Up until old Dixon got himself shot, we hadn't had murder in or about Silver City in close to five months. Now all of a sudden we got us a regular slaughter."

"Slaughter, Marshal?"

"Well, maybe that's too strong a word." McClew fired another stream of tobacco juice at the cuspidor; this one missed completely and he said, "Hell." Then he said, "Chinaman got himself hung last night. Important fella in that bunch, name of Yum Wing. You ever heard of him?"

"Yes. Will Coffin mentioned his name on the stage the other night. I also read Coffin's editorial in yesterday's *Volunteer*."

"You talk to him? Yum Wing, I mean."

Quincannon hesitated, but only for a second. "I did, yes. I thought he might know what had happened to Jason Elder."

"Because Elder was a dope fiend and old Yum Wing peddled the stuff."

"Yes."

"Did he know what had become of Elder?"

"If he did he wouldn't tell me. Who do you think killed *him*, Marshal?"

"Can't say yet. Figured maybe you'd have an idea."

"I'm sorry, I don't," Quincannon said. "Unless it was somebody who used Will Coffin's editorial as an excuse to take the law into his own hands. A very inflammatory piece of writing, wouldn't you say?"

"I would," McClew agreed. "Could have happened that way, all right. Always a few damn fool hotheads looking to make trouble. And plenty of folks don't like the Chinese because they got different ways and a different skin." He paused. "What's your feelings along them lines?"

"I think a man is a man, no matter what color his skin. I think he ought to be allowed to live his life as he sees fit, as long as he doesn't harm anyone else."

McClew seemed to approve of that. He

had himself another spit, missed his target again, and then shook his head. "Three murders inside a week," he said. "Yessir, that may not be enough to be called a slaughter, but it sure comes close enough in my book."

"*Three* murders?"

"Didn't I mention the third one? No, I guess I didn't. Sam Morant, works out at the Whiskey Gulch mine, spotted the corpse yesterday afternoon, down in a canyon off an old road ain't used much anymore. Too many rock-slides. But Sam ain't got much sense and he uses it as a shortcut to town. Anyways, he rode in and told me and I rode back out there with him and had a look. Had to leave the body where it laid, though."

"Why is that?"

"Couldn't get all the way down to it. Sheer walls and no other way into that part of the canyon. But I got close enough so's I could take a good look at him through my spyglass."

"Did you recognize him?"

"Might have, but the damned birds and coyotes had been at him, and wasn't much left of his face. Been down there close to a week, I'd say. Poor bastard. Looked like he'd been tortured some before he died."

"Tortured? What makes you say that?"

"Burn marks all over what was left of him. Kind a cigar end or the like makes on a man's flesh."

Quincannon digested this before he spoke again. "Have you any idea who the man was?"

"Well, now, I know who he was. Whoever chucked him into that canyon didn't pay enough attention to what he was doing. Or maybe it was night and he just didn't see what happened. Anyhow, some things come out of the dead man's pocket on his way down and a couple of 'em got caught up in some brush. Which is where I found 'em."

McClew opened a drawer in his desk, took out a card, and slid it over to where Quincannon could read it. It was a torn and ink-stained union card — the International Typographical Union — and the name on it was Jason Elder.

Quincannon looked up without touching the card. "I can't say I'm surprised," he said.

"Somehow I didn't figure you would be."

"Marshal, if that is an insinuation that I might have had something to do with Elder's death, I must remind you that I have only been in Silver City three days. And you yourself said that Elder's corpse has been in that canyon for close to a week."

"So I did," McClew said. "But I wasn't insinuating anything, Mr. Lyons. No sir, not me. Just trying to get to the bottom of things." He paused for another spit. "I suppose you wouldn't know anything about Elder being killed, either?"

"No more than I know about Whistling Dixon's death, or Yum Wing's."

"I figured not. Tell me, you expect to go on asking questions like you have been?"

"Not if you'd rather I didn't."

"Too many cooks spoil the broth, if you take my meaning. Besides, you ain't a lawman."

"That's right," Quincannon said, "I'm not. Very well, Marshal, I will cease and desist and leave the detecting to you."

"I'm pleased to hear you say that. How long you figuring to stay in Silver, if you don't mind saying?"

"Not much longer. My business here is about finished."

"Well, I hope you been selling plenty of nerve and brains salts. Quite a few folks around here could use some fortifying of both."

"I've been fortunate thus far."

"Yes you have," McClew said meaningfully. He watched Quincannon get on his feet. "If you should happen to hear anything I might like to know, or remember anything you might've forgot to tell me just now, you come see me again before you leave. I'll be around for you to find. And I expect the vice versa'll be true, too, if needs be."

"Just as you say, Marshal."

From behind the door to the cellblock, the man named Dewey began shouting again for his breakfast. McClew, looking put-upon, was yelling back at him, "Dewey, damn your drunken soul, if you don't shut your face I'll lock you up for a week with them women from the Temperance Union," as Quincannon went out the door.

Chapter 14

From the courthouse he made his way to the nearest saloon for whiskey. McClew was a shrewd man, he thought as he drank; there was no gainsaying that. And for all appearances, an honest one. He had been favorably impressed by the man — but he still wasn't ready to take the marshal into his confidence, not while he was on his own here. McClew's help could be solicited after Samuel Greenspan arrived. Meanwhile, he would have to be circumspect in how he conducted his investigation.

Quincannon ordered a second whiskey, which was a mistake. It made him woozy; last night's beating had weakened him more than he cared to admit. Outside again, he stood for a time in the warming wind to let his head clear. Then, still moving at a retarded pace in deference to his bruised ribs, he left the downtown area, crossed Jordan Creek, and went up

Morning Star Street.

As he walked he pondered what McClew had told him about Jason Elder. The tramp printer's death was hardly unexpected; nor was there much surprise in the fact that Elder had been tortured before he was killed. Conrad again? Bogardus? One or the other seemed likely. It was also likely that the purpose of the torture had been to force Elder to reveal the whereabouts of the item, whatever it was, that he had given to Yum Wing for safekeeping. And if Whistling Dixon had been assigned the task of disposing of Elder's corpse, it would explain how he had come by Elder's brand-new watch: he had simply removed it from the dead man's pocket before dumping the body.

Some of the pieces were beginning to fit together now. But others remained puzzling, and one of the largest of those was Helen Truax.

He turned off Morning Star toward where the Truax mansion sat on its lofty perch, looking down on the rest of Silver City. As he approached he saw that the buggy Mrs. Truax had been driving last night, with the dappled gray in harness, stood waiting before the carriage barn to one side of the main house; he took that to mean she was home. He opened the front gate, went up the path to the veranda stairs.

But he had only climbed two when a woman's voice, shrill with anger and loud enough to be heard above the pound of the stamp mills, came from inside and off to the right.

Quincannon stood still, listening. He thought he heard a man's voice, and then the woman's again, just as shrill and just as angry; but the words of both were indistinct. He backed down off the stairs, followed another path that paralleled a thick row of lilac bushes along the right side of the house. Halfway back, a pair of French windows had been opened to admit fresh air and the morning sun. The voices were coming from inside there, and when he drew closer he could hear what was being said.

". . . tell you, I won't do it!"

"Yes, you will. You'll do just as I say."

"I won't, damn you!"

There was a sharp smacking noise, flesh against flesh, followed by a small cry. Quincannon eased into the bushes on the near side of the window, poked his head over the top of one and peered through the crack where the inner edge of the window hinged outward. At first the only person he could see was Helen Truax, standing next to a mahogany music cabinet with one hand to her cheek and her eyes blazing. Quincannon moved his head slightly, to improve the field of his vision. More of the room appeared — a sitting room, filled with expensive furniture — and finally he saw the man who had struck her, in hard profile a few steps away.

It surprised him not at all that the man was Jack Bogardus.

She said, "You shouldn't have hit me, Jack. Not in my own house."

"Your house. Hell. None of this is yours; it belongs to that fat son of a bitch you married."

"You shouldn't have hit me," she said again, in the same cold, angry voice.

"I'll hit you any time I please," Bogardus said. "Here or anywhere else." He smiled at her without humor. "Besides, you know you like rough handling."

"I don't."

"You do, Helen. Same as you like me coming here while your pig of a husband is at the Paymaster. Same as you like what we do while I'm here."

"Don't talk that way. I don't like vulgar talk."

Bogardus laughed, as if she had told a particularly funny joke. He put his back to the window, went to where a cut-glass decanter and matching glasses sat on a sideboard, and poured himself a drink. When he turned again to look at Helen Truax, he also faced the window at something of an oblique angle. Quincannon lowered his head, even though Bogardus' attention was fixed on the woman.

"Well?" Bogardus said. "More argument?"

She folded her arms across her heavy breasts and hugged herself as if she might be feeling a chill. "I don't like it, Jack. Hasn't there been enough of that already?" The anger had faded from her voice; now she sounded nervous and perhaps a little afraid.

"Yes," he said. "Too much. But it can't be helped."

"Why do I have to be the one?"

"We've already discussed that."

"It has to be tonight?"

"The sooner the better."

"I don't have to stay at the mine, do I?"

"Why not? You might enjoy the game."

"Damn you, Jack. . . ."

Bogardus laughed again. He finished his drink, put the glass down, and moved over to stand in front of her. Still smiling, he slapped her a second time — not hard, but hard enough to sting.

She flushed and started to slap him in return, but he caught her wrist. She said, "What did you do that for?" with the anger in her voice again.

"I don't like to be damned. Now are you going to do as you're told?"

"All right. All right!"

"That's better."

She fingered her cheek where his hand had left a red mark. "What about that drummer?"

"I haven't made up my mind about him yet. If he keeps asking the wrong questions, he'll wish he hadn't."

"*Another* disappearance, Jack?" she said bitterly.

"Never mind that. One matter at a time. But we can't afford to let anyone stand in our way now, this close to the finish. Not anyone, you understand?"

"When will we be able to leave Silver?"

"It won't be long," Bogardus said. "Now that we're operating again, another couple of weeks is all we'll need — at least two more big shipments. Then I'll arrange to blow up the Rattling Jack, claim an accident, and we'll all leave here rich."

196

"We'll go to Europe? You promised me that."

"You sure you don't want to keep on living with that pig you married?"

"Don't toy with me, Jack. You know how I feel about you. I was a fool to walk out the way I did in Portland."

"Yes you were. But it's a good thing you did or neither of us would be in Silver right now." Bogardus rubbed her reddened cheek with the back of one hand. "All right, Helen. New York first, then Europe."

"London? Paris?"

"Anyplace you want to go."

She looked at him for a time with her eyes as dark and hot as his. Then she said softly, "Damn you, Jack. Damn you."

The words surprised Bogardus, but only for a few seconds. A slow smile lifted the corners of his mouth — and he slapped her. Not hard enough to rock her, but harder than before.

"Damn you," she said.

He slapped her again.

Her breath came faster; Quincannon could hear the irregular rhythm of it even out where he was crouched. Perspiration put a polished sheen on her flushed cheeks. "Damn you. Damn you."

Another slap, with enough force this

time so that it sounded like the crack of a pistol shot. And in the next second she was in Bogardus' arms, her hands in his black hair, her mouth hungry on his. Quincannon watched, feeling like a voyeur but unwilling to leave just yet; he was afraid of making a noise to alert them to his presence and of missing out on further conversation.

But they had nothing more to say to each other, at least not there in the sitting room and not with words. When their embrace ended, Bogardus urged her through a doorway and she went along willingly. It was obvious where they were bound. As soon as they were out of sight, Quincannon stood up out of the painful crouch he had been in, left the shelter of the lilacs, and hurried out of the yard and down away from the house. For the time being, there was nothing more to be learned there.

But his chance few minutes of eavesdropping had paid some dividends. He now had more confirmation, by implication if not by direct statement, that Bogardus and Helen Truax were involved in an illegal enterprise that almost certainly had to be the coney game. And that Bogardus considered him a potential threat, and would arrange "another disappearance" if he deemed it necessary.

The significance of the rest of their conversation, however, eluded him. What was it Bogardus had been demanding that she do tonight? What were the two of them plotting? He felt he ought to have some inkling of the answer, yet he couldn't quite grasp it. That second whiskey he had taken before going to the Truax house still had his mind fuddled. He would have to be more careful about how much and how often he drank, at least until this business was resolved.

Downtown again, he found himself on Avalanche Avenue. He glanced up at the window of Sabina's Millinery as he walked by, but he didn't hesitate; he had nothing more to say to Sabina Carpenter, not this soon after last night. At Jordan Street he turned downhill. His intended destination was Cadmon's Livery for a horse, which he would ride to the Paymaster Mine for another talk with Oliver Truax; but the Western Union sign beckoned as he passed the Wells Fargo office. He turned inside.

Waiting for him was a second telegram from Boggs, just come in from San Francisco. This one said:

SC CONFIRMED DENVER PINK ROSE ASSIGNED PMC FMFM STOP PROBABLE OT PYRAMID STOP IS THERE CONNECTION OUR BUSINESS QMK PINK ROSE RELIABLE ALLY IF JOINT VENTURE DESIRABLE OR NECESSARY

Quincannon stared at the words in amazement. Well I will be damned, he thought.

The news that the Paymaster Mining Company flimflam was a probable pyramid swindle — in which Oliver Truax would be juggling stock proceeds, paying dividends to early investors with the money from sales to later investors and then pocketing the difference — came as no surprise. It was the other revelation that astonished him, the fact that Truax and his scheme were already being investigated first-hand and undercover by a "Pink Rose."

Sabina Carpenter was an operative for the Denver branch of the Pinkerton Detective Agency.

Chapter 15

She was alone in the front part of the milli-nery shop, cutting a strip from a bolt of paisley cloth, when Quincannon turned in off the stairs. She looked up, wearing the po-lite smile of a proprietress for a prospective customer; then the smile vanished and she straightened and set down her shears. She stood stiffly, watching him.

He stopped five feet from the table. Her hair was different again today: pulled back and rolled into a tight chignon. It gave her face a severity that was enhanced by the displeasure in her expression. Neverthe-less he felt the same physical desire as last night: like it or not, she was a fire in his blood. He forced himself to remember their last meeting, the embarrassment of it; to face her with a professional detach-ment.

She said, "You have quite a nerve, Mr. Lyons, coming back here after last night. I should have thought I made it quite clear how I felt."

"You did. The purpose of this visit is strictly business."

"What sort of business?"

"The sort that needs to be discussed in complete privacy. I think you should go downstairs, put up the 'Closed' sign, and lock the door so we won't be disturbed."

She smiled wryly. "I'm sure you do."

"I assure you," he said with some of her stiffness, "that I have no intention of making any more improper advances. Your virtue is quite safe."

"Just what is it you wish to discuss?"

"Among other matters, you and your reason for coming to Silver City."

She frowned. "My reason for coming here was to open this millinery shop."

"No it wasn't," he said. "You came to prove, if you could, that Oliver Truax is operating a pyramid swindle with Paymaster Mining Company stock."

The words startled her. Some of the color faded out of her cheeks; the displeasure and the feminine righteousness faded with it, leaving her with an uncertain look. She caught her lower lip between her teeth, realized what she was doing, and released it. She didn't speak.

Quincannon said, "The fact is, Miss Carpenter, you are a Pink Rose operating out of Denver. You know what the term 'Pink Rose' means, don't you?"

She knew and she grew even paler. Her gaze held his for another second or two, then slid away. Abruptly she came away from the table, moved past him to the stairs, picked up her skirts, and hurried down. He heard her at the door, the sound of the bolt being thrown. When she came back up she returned to the table, without looking at him as she passed, and stood with one hand resting on the bolt of cloth. Her fingers, he noticed, were only inches from the sharp pair of shears.

"Your name isn't Andrew Lyons, is it," she said.

"No. It's Quincannon. John Quincannon."

"Quincannon," she repeated, as if tasting the word. "Very well, Mr. Quincannon, what is it you want from me?"

"Cooperation."

"I don't understand."

"We are more or less in the same profession, you and I," he said. "I am an operative of the United States Secret Service, attached to the field office in San Francisco."

Her eyes widened. Incredulously she said, "The Secret Service? Really, Mr. Quincannon . . ."

"You don't believe me?"

"Why should I? After all, you're a —" She broke off.

"A drunkard? Yes, Miss Carpenter, I am. And the fact will no doubt cost me my job one day." He took out his Service badge and Boggs' latest telegram, moved over to set both items on the table, and then stepped back. "Perhaps those will convince you." He waited until she had examined them, then said, "The telegram is from the agent in charge of the San Francisco office. He signs himself Arthur Caldwell, but his real name is Boggs. You can verify that by wire, if you like, through the Pinkerton office in Denver. I'm sure Mr. Boggs has been in touch with your superior there."

She seemed confused and nonplussed now, as if all of this was too much for her to grasp at once. She moved away from the table again, this time to sit down on a stool used for customer fittings. After a moment she said, "You've shaken me, Mr. Quincannon. More than I care to admit."

"It was as much of a shock for me to learn that you're a Pinkerton."

"I suppose so. But what is a Secret

Serviceman doing *here?* Not investigating Oliver Truax and the Paymaster Mining Company, surely . . ."

"No. A gang of counterfeiters is what I'm after."

"Coneymen? In Silver City?"

"Yes. One of the largest and most organized boodle games ever to operate west of the Rocky Mountains."

"Do you know who is running it?"

"I have strong suspicions, yes."

"It's not Oliver Truax?"

"No. I don't believe he's involved. But I do think his wife might be."

That surprised the Pink Rose, but not as much as it might have. She said, "How would Helen Truax be mixed up with counterfeiters?"

"Jack Bogardus," he said.

"You mean you suspect Bogardus is the ringleader?"

"I do. And that the Rattling Jack mine is the manufacturing and shipping point for the queer."

She nodded slowly and thoughtfully. "Yes, I can see how that might be possible. Do you have proof?"

"Not quite enough to act on as yet. I take it you had no suspicions anything of the sort might be going on?"

"No, none. It's common knowledge that Mrs. Truax and Bogardus are engaged in a clandestine relationship; I have even seen the two of them together. But I believed, as everyone else does, that Bogardus' new-found wealth was the result of a rich new silver vein."

"Whistling Dixon was involved, too," Quincannon said. "I believe that's why he was killed. And the same is true of Jason Elder."

"Elder is dead?"

"Yes. His body was found yesterday, in a canyon back in the hills. He had been tortured before he was killed."

"My God. Why?"

"He had something Bogardus and his gang badly wanted; I'm not sure what. But he wouldn't tell them what he'd done with it even under the torture. They thought he might have hidden it at the newspaper office or given it to Will Coffin; that is why the office and Coffin's house were broken into, not because of any Chinese retaliation against his stand on opium. They also searched Elder's shack, of course. It *was* ransacked before you searched it yourself?"

"Yes. I thought it strange when I found it that way."

"Why were you at Elder's shack?"

"Last week I followed Mrs. Truax there — a curious rendezvous for a woman of her station. I intended to investigate her relationship with Elder, but then I learned Oliver Truax was going to Boise to sell a block of Paymaster stock and I followed him there instead. Tuesday morning was the first opportunity I had to check up on Elder. And it seemed safe enough to search his shack then; I ran into Will Coffin before I went there and he told me Elder had disappeared."

"Where did you find the stock certificate?"

"In a fireproof box inside the stove."

"Was there anything else in the box?"

She shook her head. "Is it possible the certificate is what Bogardus was after?"

"I don't see how. Do you?"

"No," she said. "There is nothing important or incriminating about it that I can see. Still . . . she *was* eager enough to have it back when she confronted me."

"*She* confronted *you*? Didn't you tell her on Tuesday night that you had found the certificate?"

"I did not. I had struck up an acquaintance with the woman and invited her to visit the shop." There was reproof in Sabina Carpenter's tone as she said, "You were the one who told her I had the stock."

"A foolish mistake," Quincannon admitted, "and I apologize for it. What was her mood when she came to you about it?"

"Angry, of course. She demanded that I let her have the certificate."

"Did you give it to her?"

"I had no choice. She threatened to go to the marshal if I didn't."

"Do you know why she signed her stock over to Elder?"

"No. She wouldn't say, and I had no luck finding out on my own. I couldn't imagine a personal relationship between her and Elder. You never saw him, did you? He was an ugly little man with yellow skin from his addiction. But now I wonder if it was something to do with the boodle game that caused her to give him the stock."

"It must have been."

"You suspect Elder of being the engraver of the counterfeit plates?"

"Yes," Quincannon said, and something stirred in his memory — something he had overheard Bogardus say to Helen Truax. *Now that we're operating again, another couple of weeks is all we'll need — at least two more big shipments.*

Now that we're operating again . . .

"The plates," he said.

Sabina Carpenter looked at him questioningly.

"The plates," he repeated. "God, yes, *that* must be what Elder hid from Bogardus. There was a falling out of some sort, Elder took the plates, Bogardus tried to buy them back with Mrs. Truax's Paymaster stock and when that didn't work, he resorted to torture that went too far."

"That does sound reasonable," she said. There was animation in her voice now that her initial shock and confusion had gone. An excitement, too — the kind that had once been in him when a difficult and intriguing case was about to break wide open. "But where could Elder have hidden the plates?"

"He didn't hide them; he gave them to his opium supplier, Yum Wing, for safekeeping."

"Of course! Yum Wing's death last night — Bogardus was responsible for that?"

Quincannon dipped his chin affirmatively. "I was almost able to prevent it," he said, "but I realized the truth too late. Yum Wing was already dead when I arrived. His killers jumped me from hiding; they mistook me for another Chinese in the dark or they would probably have murdered me, too."

"That explains the cut on your head — I've been wondering about that." She paused. "Do you think they got the plates?"

"I'm certain they did," Quincannon said. He explained what he had overheard at the Truax house.

"What will you do now?" she asked. "It seems to me you have sufficient proof against Bogardus to take direct action."

"To me as well. But Mr. Boggs and the gentlemen in Washington are much more cautious in these matters than either of us."

"I know what you mean. The man I work for in Denver, James Lumley, is the same sort. Which is why I'm still operating this shop and Oliver Truax is still a free man."

"You have evidence of Truax's guilt, then?"

"Considerable evidence."

"A pyramid swindle?"

"Exactly. The man is riddled with greed, and reckless because of it. He will sell any amount of Paymaster stock to any interested party for immediate payment in cash. He told me there were no shares available for sale when I first approached him, but when I showed him the Agency's five thousand dollars, I owned a hundred shares less than twenty-four hours later."

"He tried the same ploy on me," Quincannon said, "when I approached him on behalf of the owner of my fictitious patent medicine company."

"Then you see what I mean. Bold as brass. The reason he went to Boise was to sell five hundred shares to a banker there; I got wind of the deal and arranged for a witness to the exchange. And still Mr. Lumley and our clients want more proof to insure a conviction."

"Who are your clients?"

"A group of Paymaster investors. They began to suspect the swindle a few weeks ago."

Quincannon nodded, and a momentary silence settled between them. A shaft of sunlight slanting in through the window touched her hair, making it glisten with reddish highlights. He felt the physical desire again, rebuked himself sharply, and looked away from her.

"May I ask you a personal question, Miss Carpenter?"

"That depends on the question."

"How do you happen to work for Pinkerton?"

She smiled faintly. "Do you hold a prejudice against women operatives, Mr. Quincannon?"

"None whatsoever. I met Allan Pinkerton's first female employee, Kate Warne, on a case in Chicago some years ago and found her highly competent. But I confess to curiosity: detective work is not an ordinary job for a woman."

"My husband was an operative for the Denver agency," she said. "One of its best, I may say."

"Was?"

"He was killed while on a land-fraud case two years ago." She spoke the words matter-of-factly, but he detected traces of bitterness and lingering grief. "Shot to death during a raid."

"So was my father," Quincannon said. "Several years ago on the Baltimore docks. He was a detective, too, a rival of Pinkerton's."

There was a space before she spoke again; her eyes, steady on his now, held a look of what he took to be compassion and a sense of kinship. He felt that he wanted to go to her, touch her, but he was afraid she might misinterpret any such intimacy as another improper advance.

"Birds of a feather," she said. "Lonely birds, always on the wing — targets for a hunter's gun."

It was an odd phrase, vaguely haunting,

and it invited no reply.

She asked, "You are lonely, aren't you, Mr. Quincannon? I sense it in you. Is that why you took to whiskey?"

"No."

"Then why? Is it because of the woman I resemble?"

The conversation had become too personal; her questions made him feel ill at ease, brought Katherine Bennett back into his consciousness. He said, "I had better leave now. There are things to be done."

"Yes. Of course."

He turned for the stairs, stopped after two paces, and faced her again. "How late do you expect to be here tonight?"

"Until about six."

"I wonder . . . if I came back then, would you consider taking supper with me?"

The faint smile again. "Do you intend to kiss me again afterward?"

"No," he said. And then, on impulse, "Does it offend you that I find you an attractive woman?"

"I should be offended if you didn't."

He laughed and so did she, spontaneously, and his feeling of awkwardness and unease vanished. She had a fine, rich laugh; he thought that it would be good to hear it more often. "At six then, Miss Carpenter?"

"Very well, Mr. Quincannon — at six."

"John, if you will."

"Sabina."

Downstairs, he switched the sign on the door glass so that it read OPEN facing forward, then unlocked the door and went out. The meeting with Sabina Carpenter had gone far better than he had anticipated. He felt almost cheerful, almost human again — the first time he had experienced such normal feelings since Virginia City. He neither needed nor wanted a drink, and that too was an odd new feeling.

On Washington Street he went down across the creek toward Cadmon's Livery. It was still his intention to rent a horse, but no longer to visit Oliver Truax; he was convinced, after his talk with Sabina, that Truax was much too involved in his own illegal enterprise to be mixed up in the coney game. Quincannon's aim this time was the Rattling Jack and any sort of flaw in its fortresslike defenses.

But what he saw when he neared the livery diverted that aim for the present and gave him a different purpose. A yellow Studebaker freight wagon was drawn up in front of the entrance, its deep bed covered with canvas — the same wagon and the same team, he was sure, that Jack Bogardus had brought from Truax two days ago. Its burly driver was up on the high seat, engaged in some sort of argument with the liveryman named Henry. The man's slablike face was turned so that Quincannon could see it and the thatch of fiery red hair that topped it.

Both were familiar, unmistakably so. The driver of the Rattling Jack freight wagon was the man who had murdered Quincannon's informant, Bonniwell, in San Francisco.

Chapter 16

It was doubtful the red-haired man had got a good look at him in return that night, shielded as he'd been by the rain and darkness, but Quincannon turned quickly aside and detoured over toward the blacksmith's shop beyond the livery. He needn't have worried. The redhead was intent on his argument with Henry and for the moment oblivious to his surroundings. Quincannon stopped under the drooping branches of a willow that fronted the blacksmith's, directly behind the wagon and close enough to hear what the two men were arguing about.

"How the hell you expect me to get this ore down the mountain with a spavined horse *and* a cracked doubletree?" the redhead was saying. "I wouldn't make it halfway to the Poison Creek station."

"Is that my fault?" Henry said. "I told you, Griswold, I ain't got a doubletree for

216

that kind of rig. Why don't you try Tully's place?"

"I already did on the way in. Can't you make one?"

"Couldn't Tully?"

"Said it'd take him all afternoon."

"Well, it would me, too."

"I tell you, I got to get this load to Boise," the redhead, Griswold, said. "Listen, how about repairing the doubletree. You can do that, can't you?"

"I suppose I could," Henry said grudgingly. "Piece of scrap iron might do it. But I couldn't give you any guarantee she'd hold up."

"I ain't asking for any guarantee."

"Hell, I don't know. I got other work to do. . . ."

Griswold said, "I'll pay you an extra twenty if you get me on the road by two o'clock."

"Twenty dollars, you say?"

"A brand-new greenback. Well?"

"All right, then. Pull the wagon inside and I'll see what I can do."

Henry stepped back and the red-haired man brought the team around, drove the Studebaker up the ramp and into the shadowed interior of the livery. When Henry had gone in after it, Quincannon left the shade of the willow. He wanted a look at the "ore" in the wagon, but he was not about to get it with both Griswold and Henry in there. What he had to do was find a way to get them out of the building for a time.

He moved along the south wall, around to the rear. There was a back entrance, he saw, a single door that he surmised would lead in among the horse stalls. He stood for a moment, scanning the area. Out here were a good-sized manure pile, some patches of dry sage and grass, the skeletons of two abandoned wagons, and more sage-brush climbing the slope beyond. There was nobody around. And once he had taken half a dozen steps toward the ma-nure pile, the entrance to the blacksmith's, from which he could smell the sharp odors of burning coal and hot metal, was no longer visible.

The droppings around the edge of the pile were dry; quickly, using the side of his boot, he scraped some of them into a sepa-rate mound in a big patch of dead grass, twenty feet or so from the back wall of the livery. Then he pulled up handfuls of sage and grass and added them to the mound. The wind was gusty, blowing down from the higher elevations; he put his back to it, so as to shield his hands, and scraped a match alight. Within seconds the dry grass and sage began to blaze. And when the droppings caught, the smoke that poured up from the fire thickened and was wind-driven against the livery.

Quincannon went to the rear door, pounded on it urgently, and yelled, "Fire! Fire!"

Inside, voices and running steps responded. He ducked around the north corner, ran as fast as his bruised ribs would allow to the front entrance. From there he could see the Studebaker wagon and the floor space around it: there was no sign of Henry or the redhead. The rear door must be open — he could smell smoke from the fire, see trailing wisps of it in the lamplit interior. At a distance, someone — it sounded like Henry — was cursing inventively.

Quincannon ran up the ramp, across to the tailgate of the Studebaker, and loosened one of the ropes that secured the canvas covering the bed. Under the canvas, he saw when he lifted the corner flap, were a dozen or so wood-slat crates. He tugged at the top of the nearest crate, found that it had been nailed down. But there was finger space between two of the slats; he got a grip on one and wrenched once, twice, three times before a nail pulled loose and part of the slat splintered off with a loud snapping noise.

He jerked his head up to look toward the rear. But the sound had been lost among several others. The horses back there had smelled the fire and were making nervous snorts and thumpings in their stalls; the drays harnessed to the Studebaker were likewise being noisily skittish. Outside Henry was still yelling. It was plain that he and Griswold were still occupied in trying to put out the fire.

Quincannon shoved his hand down through the broken section of the box lid, felt straw packing, and burrowed through it. His fingers touched something — paper, a small bundle — and then caught hold of it and dragged it out into the light. The bundle was of brand-new greenbacks, twenties judging from the top one, tied with thin twine. He pushed it into his coat pocket, dropped the canvas and retied the rope, and hurriedly backed away from the wagon.

No one saw him leave the livery except a group of three men who had been drawn by the smoke and were on their way around back; none of them paid any attention to him. A short distance away, he paused to check the bundle of greenbacks more closely; they were definitely counterfeit. Then he continued uphill at a rapid pace, but after a block, pain from his ribs and shortness of breath forced him into a walk. He was sweating and dry-mouthed by the time he reached the Wells Fargo building.

At the Western Union counter he composed a lengthy wire to Boggs. Added to the proof he had already assembled, the bogus notes in his pocket and his positive identification of Griswold as Bonniwell's killer gave him all the justification he needed to take direct action. There was no doubt now that Bogardus was the leader of the koniakers, and that the Rattling Jack was where the queer was being manufactured. Even Boggs, once he had all the data in hand, would be satisfied of that.

He requested that federal arrest and search-and-seizure warrants be obtained, and the immediate dispatching to Silver City of as many federal officers as could be spared. He also requested that a watch be put on the wagon road between Silver and Boise and when the Studebaker wagon arrived, Griswold be placed under arrest and the shipment of counterfeit confiscated. If

Boggs wasted no time when the telegram arrived — and he wouldn't, knowing Boggs — the necessary men and papers should all be here within three days. A raid on the Rattling Jack could be mounted sometime on Sunday, then, preferably with the assistance of Marshal McClew and as many special deputies as he could provide.

Quincannon waited until the message was sent, then found his way to Silver's other livery stable, Tully's, where he rented both a spyglass and a claybank horse with a placid disposition. For his mission to the Rattling Jack, he wanted an animal that wouldn't fuss when it was left alone in unfamiliar territory and thereby call attention to itself and to him.

On his way out of town he rode by Cadmon's Livery, venturing close enough to determine that the red-haired man and the Studebaker wagon were still there. It was already two o'clock; because of the fire, Griswold would be even later starting down the Poison Creek road on his way to Boise. All the more time for federal officers to establish watchpoints on the road leading into the state capital.

Near Ruby City Quincannon took the narrow wagon road that led around to the south slope of War Eagle Mountain. Wind lashed at him as he passed through the hollows and over the swells toward the Rattling Jack. The jouncing gait of the horse aggravated the pain along his rib cage; twice he had to stop for short periods to ease it and to catch his breath. When he neared the turning beyond where the mine buildings clung to the hillside he left the road and found a way down through the ravine below. The terrain soon roughened and became so rocky that he had to step down and lead the claybank, upslope in one place around an old prospect hole.

It took half an hour for him to work his way to within a hundred yards of the stockade fence. There he ground-reined the horse and went on foot to the fence, along it stealthily for a short distance in two directions. As he had suspected, there were no openings large enough for a man to pass through; and climbing it would be a damned difficult proposition, for the posts were made of juniper stakes sharpened to points at the top. The only feasible way in, aside from storming the gates, was from the bluff at the rear — *if* the bluff face could be scaled.

He returned to the claybank, mounted, and swung back along the ravine until he found a place where he could climb out on the east side, beyond the mine. Then he headed back to the south, up onto the bluff. At a point where the Rattling Jack was still hidden, he again ground-reined the horse, took the rented spyglass, and went on foot to the scattered rocks along the edge. He settled himself behind an outcrop, from where he had a clear overall view of the compound below.

Through the glass he studied the surface works. The building nearest the bluff was also the largest in the compound: the main shaft house. Below it to the west was a stone-walled powder magazine, the tramway, and at the foot of the slope, the stamp mill. On the east side were a stable, a pair of frame structures that were probably living quarters, and the mine office. The rest of the yard was cluttered with wagons, tools, a lean-to used for storage, and a long rick of mine timbers.

Although the stamps were pounding way inside the mill, sending up jets of smoke and steam through the roof stacks, the tram was deserted again today. There was no watchman on the gates; evidently Bogardus felt the fence was sufficient security. Men moved here and there in the yard at irregular intervals, and the building that drew and disgorged most of them was the largest and furthest uphill of the two bunk-houses.

Was that where the counterfeit notes were being made? It seemed a good bet. They would need plenty of room for the printing press, the bundles of paper and the different types of ink, the containers of acid and powdered resin, all the other items an operation of this size and production required. And none of the other buildings in the compound seemed suitable. The manufacturing point of the silver eagles and half eagles, on the other hand, was probably the stamp mill, where they would have ready access to the silver that came out of the stamps.

At length Quincannon lowered the glass and looked down the face of the bluff. The drop-off was almost vertical, and at the bottom were buildups of talus and loose dirt; but it could be scaled by an agile man using a strong rope under the cover of darkness. A night raid, then — it would have to be. One man to get in this way, when the koniakers were asleep, and then open the gate to let in the rest. With a modicum of luck, the whole operation could be accomplished without a shot being fired.

Satisfied, he segmented the glass and made his way back to where he had left the claybank. He retraced his route to the ravine and through to the wagon road on the west side of the mine, so that it was as fixed in his mind as the layout of the compound. He would have no trouble leading the raiding party here when the time came.

It was after five when he arrived back in Silver City. In his room at the hotel, where he went directly after returning the claybank to Tully's Livery, he shucked out of his dusty clothes and lay down on the bed to rest. Fatigue was heavy in him; his side ached and there was a dull throbbing in his head. Too much whiskey this morning, too much exertion this afternoon. And too much manhandling last night.

But his need for rest was exceeded by his desire to see Sabina again. He roused himself after half an hour, washed, combed his hair, and put on fresh clothing from his warbag. His stemwinder gave the time as five past six when he left the hotel. The thought of a drink was in his mind as he walked toward Avalanche Avenue, but he did not want to see her tonight with whiskey on his breath. And he still didn't seem to need it or its numbing effect. Later, no doubt, but not just now.

When he reached the millinery shop he saw that no lamp burned behind its window. The sun was gone and twilight was beginning to settle; if she was here waiting for him she should have lighted the lamp by now.

But she wasn't here: the door was locked.

Had she changed her mind about having dinner with him? Or left when he failed to arrive promptly at six? He didn't believe either possibility. She was not the type of woman who made petty decisions based on emotional whim; she was a Pink Rose. She had said she would wait here for him. She should be here waiting.

An uneasiness moved through him. He turned toward the lighted barbershop and hurried inside. The barber, a tall man with muttonchop whiskers, was just taking off his apron, getting ready to close for the day. Quincannon asked him if he had seen Sabina Carpenter leave her shop upstairs.

"Yes, sir, so happens I did," the barber said. "I was shaving a customer at the time and noticed her through the window."

"What time was that?"

"Oh, half an hour, forty-five minutes ago."

"Was she alone?"

"No, sir. She was with Oliver Truax's wife. Two of them rode off in Mrs. Truax's buggy."

Helen Truax. Sabina and Helen Truax.

And then he understood; the knowledge came to him with a suddenness that was jarring, followed by a wave of anxiety and self-hatred. He should have understood long before this. If he had, this wouldn't have happened at all. His fault. It was *his* fault if any harm came to her.

What he had overheard Bogardus and Helen Truax plotting this morning, what he had stupidly failed to grasp at the time, was Sabina's abduction and eventual murder.

Chapter 17

He ran out of the barbershop, across the rutted avenue toward Jordan Street. A keg-laden wagon from the local brewery almost ran him down; the driver reined his team aside just in time, hurled a string of curses at Quincannon's back. He barely noticed. His head was full of the words Bogardus and Helen Truax had spoken this morning, words that fairly screamed their significance to him now.

I don't like it, Jack. Hasn't there been enough of that already?

Yes. Too much. But it can't be helped.

Why do I have to be the one?

We've already discussed that.

It has to be tonight?

The sooner the better.

I don't have to stay at the mine, do I?

Why not? You might enjoy the game. . . .

Another disappearance, Jack?

Never mind that. One matter at a time. But

we can't afford to let anyone stand in our way now, this close to the finish. Not anyone, you understand?

They hadn't been discussing him; it *had* to be Sabina. His fault. He'd told Helen Truax about Sabina finding the stock certificate and then hiding the fact; he'd made her realize Sabina knew about her connection with Jason Elder, made her suspicious of Sabina's motives. Naturally they wanted to know what her game was. And when they found out — or even if they didn't — Sabina would die. His fault. If he'd kept his Goddamned mouth shut, if the whiskey he'd consumed that night hadn't loosened his tongue, her life would not be in danger now.

The whiskey. It was the whiskey, too, that had kept him from realizing the sense of what he'd overheard at the Truax house. Damn the stuff, befuddling his mind and his judgment. . . .

A steady consumption of liquor distorts a man's judgment, slows his reflexes, makes him prone to mistakes.

I won't make any mistakes.

Different voices echoing in his memory, Boggs' and his own in San Francisco last week.

I won't make any mistakes. . . .

230

The irony of it was bitter, appalling. He had taken to drink to drown the horror of what he had done to Katherine Bennett, an innocent woman; and now the drink in turn had caused him to place the life of another innocent woman in jeopardy. He couldn't allow it to happen again, he could not bear the awful burden of responsibility for a second woman's death — a woman, in spite of her resemblance to Katherine Bennett, he found himself caring more about than any he had known except his mother. He would rather die himself, here tonight. If anything happened to Sabina he *would* die tonight — at the hands of Bogardus and his men, or if he survived them, by his own hand later on.

He crossed Jordan Street, cut through an alley to Washington. There was little doubt where Sabina had been taken: the Rattling Jack. Once Helen Truax, the Judas, had driven her out of town, Bogardus or some of his men would have been waiting to accompany them to the mine; there would be no escape for Sabina either from them or from the compound. A half hour to forty-five minutes ago. They would just about be arriving now. And it would not take long for one man, or several, to torture a defenseless woman, or do even worse to her.

I don't have to stay at the mine, do I?
Why not? You might enjoy the game. . . .

Quincannon's emotions urged him to run straight to the nearest livery for a horse and then to ride hell-bent for the Rattling Jack. But his intellect demanded otherwise. The chances were good that he could get inside the compound without being seen, down the bluff at the rear; but what then? How could he free Sabina and then get both of them safely out and back to town? One man pitted against a dozen or so was suicidal. No, he had to have men to back him up, men to tilt the odds in his and Sabina's favor. He couldn't wait for federal officers and the proper legal papers to arrive; he had to have a raiding party now, tonight, within two hours.

Prepared for it or not, he had to put his faith in Marshal Wendell McClew.

Darkness was fast approaching; he could see the lighted basement window of the marshal's office half a block away. Pain from his battered ribs had him gasping for breath when he finally reached the door. He threw it open, half-stumbled down the stairs.

McClew had been tacking a wanted dodger onto a wall filled with them, using the butt of his Colt six-gun for a hammer. He swung around and said in surprise,

"What the bloody bedamned! You look all het up, Mr. Lyons."

"My name isn't Lyons." The words came out in sharp little exhalations, like puffs of steam from an overworked engine. "It's Quincannon — John Quincannon. I'm an operative for the United States Secret Service."

"The United . . . *what?*"

"Secret Service. Listen to me, now, don't interrupt."

Quickly, trying to catch his breath between sentences, Quincannon explained what he was doing in Silver City and what he had learned; who Sabina Carpenter was and what she was doing here; the urgency of matters as they now stood. McClew's eyes grew wider and wider; his amazement seemed genuine. So did his skepticism.

"That's quite a yarn," he said when Quincannon was finished. "You have any proof to back it up?"

Quincannon was still carrying the bundle of bogus greenbacks he had lifted from the Studebaker wagon; he hadn't wanted to leave it in his hotel room earlier. He also had Boggs' wires and his Service badge. He put these items on McClew's desk and waited impatiently while the marshal examined the badge, read over the wires, then squinted at the queer twenties.

"Counterfeit, all right," McClew said, holding up one of the notes to the wall lamp. "Seen a few in my time; these here is good but not quite good enough." He put the bill down, tapped the badge with one of his blunt forefingers. "This looks genuine, though. I reckon I got to believe you're who you say you are."

"Can I count on your help, then?"

McClew nodded, spat tobacco juice in the general direction of the cuspidor alongside his desk. "But I sure as hell wish you'd come to me right off. Makes my job a whole lot easier when folks trust me and tell me the truth."

"I had to be certain of your honesty first," Quincannon said.

McClew wasn't offended. "Suppose you did," he said and spat again. "Bogardus, huh? Well, I never did like that son of a bitch. Nor Ollie Truax and that tramp he married. Give me pleasure to haul the lot of 'em in."

Quincannon asked, "How many special deputies can you gather on short notice?"

"Dozen or more, I expect. Maybe six or eight'll be experienced; others're liable to stoke up on Dutch courage. But I can keep 'em in line."

"How soon can you have a posse ready to ride?"

"Hour, hour and a half."

"As fast as you can, then. I'll go ahead; I'm fairly certain I can get inside the compound without being seen — by rope down the bluff at the rear."

McClew looked dubious. "What can you do in there alone?"

"Find out where they're holding Miss Carpenter," Quincannon told him, "and keep her from harm if I can. And I'll open the stockade gates for you and your men."

"Makes sense," McClew admitted. "I ain't going to argue; no time for it and I see your mind's made up. All right. Me and my men get to the Rattling Jack, then what?"

"How well do you know the terrain out there?"

"Better'n you ever will, son."

Quincannon nodded. "Leave your horses in the draw and come on foot to the fence. if the gates are unlocked, go ahead inside — quiet if you can, shooting if you have to."

"And if he gates ain't unlocked?"

"Don't wait more than half an hour. If the gates aren't open by then I won't be alive to open them."

"Good a plan as any. You got a horse handy?"

"No."

"Take mine, then. Big grulla, tied out back of the courthouse; he won't give you no trouble. Loop of good saddle rope on him, too. I'll get me another horse at Cadmon's."

Neither man wasted any more words or time. They went outside together, parted there in silence, and Quincannon ran around behind the courthouse to where the marshal's grulla was picketed. He mounted and kicked the horse into a run, west out of Silver into the wind-swept darkness beyond.

Chapter 18

The ride out to the Rattling Jack seemed in-
terminable. Restless clouds kept the moon
hidden most of the time, and the darkness
lay thick and cold over the rumpled terrain;
he was forced to slow McClew's grulla to a
walk on the rutted and rubble-strewn wagon
road. The last thing he could afford was to
have the horse stumble and break a leg —
maybe throw him and break *his* leg.

He met no one on the road. Helen
Truax, despite her protestations to
Bogardus this morning, had evidently remained at the mine; the timing was such
that he would have seen her buggy if she'd
left after delivering Sabina. It was just as
well. Avoiding her or confronting her out
here — either one — would have cost him
valuable time.

A few scattered lights in the distance told
him he was finally nearing the Rattling Jack.
He found the way down into the ravine, let

the grulla pick its way along below the mine, and then climbed out and up onto the bluff. He dismounted a hundred yards from the rim and tied the horse to a juniper bush. McClew's saddle rope was a new, strong hemp, maybe fifty feet of it. Too short to reach all the way to the bottom of the bluff face; this afternoon he had judged the drop at sixty feet or better. But there was nothing to be done about that now.

Carrying the rope, he moved ahead onto the rocks along the edge and hunkered there to study the compound. There were lights in the two bunkhouse buildings; another glowed dimly inside the main shaft house. The yard itself was in heavy shadow and looked empty — no watchman posted tonight, either. Near the stockade gates were the lumpish shapes of a horse and buggy, no doubt Helen Truax's rig. Bogardus' false sense of security would be his undoing, Quincannon thought.

Quincannon knelt among the rocks for a few seconds more, watching and listening. With the mill shut down, the night was hushed; indistinct sounds drifted up to him — horses moving about in the stable, men moving about and making noise in the bunkhouses. Outside, there was only stillness.

He worked out a loop in one end of the rope, found an upthrust knob of granite, and tied the loop around it. When he yanked on the rope, using his full strength, it held firm; the rock was anchored solidly enough to support his weight. He played the rest of the rope down the bluff wall, wound part of its upper end twice around his right leg and once around his right hand. Then he checked the compound again, made sure his revolver was tight in its holster, and swung out.

The descent was slow, arduous work — a drop of a few feet at a time, so as not to burn his hands on the rope and lose his grip; brake with his bootsoles braced against the rock wall; rest, and repeat the process. The strain on his arms and legs was acute; sweat flowed on him despite the chill plateau wind. By the time he neared the end of the rope he was short of breath again and his right side was afire.

With only a few feet of the rope left, he rested and looked down. Still more than a dozen feet to the jumble of talus and loose dirt at the base. Off to the left was the best place to make his fall — more dirt there than rock. He shoved out that way, dropped to the rope's end, straightened his body against the bluff face, and let go.

He was angled forward, waving his arms for balance, when his boots struck the loose dirt. He felt himself sliding downward, tried to throw his body down belly-flat so he could help brake his momentum with his hands; but his foot struck a heavy piece of talus and pitched him sideways, toppled him and sent him rolling over twice before he fetched up among the rubble at the bottom. The noise of dislodged rocks and his own tumbling body seemed loud in his ears. He was aware of that far more than the pain in his ribs and the scrapes and cuts from the sharp-edged talus as he dragged himself to his feet.

He pawed at his holster, felt the butt of the Remington still lodged there, and broke into a stumbling run toward the main shaft house. He saw nothing in the yard before reaching its shadowed wall, but voices came to him from somewhere beyond, carried on the wind.

". . . Thought I heard something back there."

"Hell. Nothing but the wind."

"Wasn't the wind. Sounded like somebody moving around up by the shaft house."

"Phantoms, Conrad. Ghosts and goblins."

"Stay here, then, you smart bastard. I'll go have a look myself. . . ."

Quincannon thought: Damn them! If they came back here with a lantern, he was done for. He might be able to hide from them in the darkness, but that rope hanging down the cliff face was a dead giveaway. . . .

He groped around on the east side of the shaft house, away from the sound of the voices. Open ground beyond — nowhere for him to go there. The footsteps of the two men were audible now, coming closer; but they didn't have a lantern, not yet, or he would have seen its shimmer against the blackness. He kept moving, feeling the wall with his hands.

Doorway, with its thick slab of a door pulled shut. He located the latch, opened the door just wide enough to slip his body through, and shut it soundlessly behind him.

A lighted lantern hanging to one side of a steam hoist let him see most of the big gloomy interior. There was no place for him to hide; he realized that at once. Off to his left, the boiler loomed dark and bulky, with pockets of heavy shadow around it; but if they came inside, and it seemed probable they would, that was one of the first places they would look. He couldn't get down into the main shaft, either. Its eye was blocked by the lifting cage, and starting the hoist was out of the question.

He ran toward the far end of the building. A mine of this size had to have an emergency shaft that would also serve as ventilation for the network of drifts and adits and winzes below. He found it — an opening some three feet in diameter, with a low framework of timbers around it as a safeguard against accident. An in-draft of cool air came out of it; its dank smell blended with the odors of warm grease and steam escaping from the boiler.

Sounds came to him from outside a second door, opposite the one through which he had entered. Hastily Quincannon climbed over the protective framework, found the cleats fastened to one side of the shaft. As he did, a trick of his mind brought back to him an old miners' saying. *When you step across the shaft collar you're gambling with death.* But he had no choice. He was trapped here either way. He swung his body into the opening and started down.

The trapped feeling intensified as he lowered himself into the heavy blackness. But he kept moving as fast as he dared;

they must be in the building by now, and it would not take them long to investigate this shaft. Whether or not they came down themselves depended on how spooked Conrad was.

It was a good fifty feet before he reached the first drift. He stepped off the last of the cleats, stood aside peering up toward the collar; he could barely make out the opening, a faint grayness against the deeper black. He stood still, listening. Nothing but silence for a time. Then he heard the voices again, indistinct murmurs at first that grew louder and became clearer as the men approached the shaft. He took a blind, shuffling step sideways, fingers groping against the cold rock; he did not want to move any farther away from the shaft, not unless it became necessary, for fear of bumping into tools and equipment that might have been left in the drift.

"Nobody's in here either, I tell you."

"Be quiet. Listen."

Silence for several seconds. Quincannon stood motionless, forcing himself to breathe shallowly and inaudibly through his mouth.

"You satisfied now? Who the hell would want to come in here and go down inside the mine?"

"I don't know. But with that woman here . . ."

"Yeah, that woman. I don't like that."

"Then don't think about it."

"Just the same, I don't like it. I need a drink. You coming or not?"

No answer from Conrad. Silence settled again, so thick and clotted that it was like a continual soundless scream. Quincannon thought that they had moved away from the shaft collar, maybe left the building, but there was no way to tell. He stayed where he was, waiting, sweating, listening to the silence.

Five minutes. Ten. Or maybe it was only five after all; down here in the clotted black, the passage of time was difficult to gauge. If they had gone outside and checked the bluff wall and seen the rope, they would already have sounded an alarm and the compound would be swarming with men. When they didn't find him they would come in here again and take the cage down one level at a time. There would be no escape for him then, no way to fight them; they knew the mine and its maze of drifts and crosscuts and he didn't.

The feeling of trapped panic welled in him again. He couldn't stay down here, not any longer. Sabina — Christ knew what

Bogardus might be doing to her.

He felt his way back to the cleats, began to climb them through the close confines of the shaft. Sweat made his fingers slippery around the metal; it was a constant strain to keep his labored breathing inaudible. Above him, the shaft collar grew more distinct, a lighter gray, a dull yellow. He paused a few feet below it, wiped his hands dry, and drew his revolver. Then he eased up the rest of the way, poked his head out for a quick, furtive look around.

The building appeared empty.

He climbed out and over the framework, stood for a moment to let his mind and body adjust to the release of the claustrophobic tension. When he reached the main door he edged it open. There was nothing to hear outside except for the faint skirling of the wind, the distant snorting of a restless horse. Trap? he thought. But that was foolish; if Conrad and the other man had sounded an alarm, they would have come after in full force, not be waiting for him to come to them. He opened the door wider, saw nothing to keep him inside, and slipped out.

The chill wind dried his sweat, raised gooseflesh on his arms and back as he moved along the shaft house wall. From the far corner his view of both bunkhouses and the stockade gates was obstructed by a pair of ore wagons and the rick of mine timbers. He ran across to the stack, went around the near side. Then he could see the gates; Helen Truax's buggy was no longer there and he spied it nowhere else in this vicinity. Nor was there any sign yet of a watchman.

He edged forward until he could look past the downhill side of the rick, toward the bunkhouses. The bigger of the two, the one in which he judged the counterfeiting was being done, showed strong light in its single window. The one farther downhill was also lighted and a man stood in front of it, smoking, the tip of his cigarette making a winking orange hole in the darkness.

Quincannon waited until the man finished his smoke, flicked the butt away, and went back inside. He was torn between two needs: to find out where Sabina was being held and determine if she was all right; and to unlock the gates in preparation for the arrival of McClew and his posse. His concern for Sabina's welfare was paramount. He hastened back around the uphill side of the stack, paused at its opposite end to reconnoiter the bunkhouses. There was movement behind the window in the near one, then it became a blank yellow eye again. No one was outside that he could see.

The moon came out from behind the scudding clouds, bathed the yard in its brilliance for a few moments. When it vanished again he left the timbers, moving in a crouch, and ran over behind a jumble of discarded machinery, from there into the shadows cast by the stockade fence. That put him behind the nearest bunkhouse, at an angle to its uphill rear corner. He worked his way over there, up on the balls of his feet. At the side wall he flattened his back against the boards and stood listening.

Murmurs from inside, imperceptible. Ten feet ahead, the radiance from within spilled through a side window. Quincannon inched toward it, stopped just before he reached its frame. The murmurs were louder here, but of what was being said he could make out no more than one word in ten. He crouched, moved closer to the window, then raised up until he had a sidewise view through the grime-streaked glass.

The first thing he saw was the printing press. No wonder their counterfeit was of high quality; the press was not one of the old-fashioned single-plate, hand-roller variety, but rather a steam-powered Milligan press that would perform the printing, inking, and wiping simultaneously through the continuous movement of four plates around a square frame. Along with its accessories — bundles of paper, tins of ink, a long workbench laden with tools and chemicals — the press took up most of the forward half of the single room.

Quincannon dropped low again, duck-walked under the sill, and stretched up on the window's far side so he could see into the back half of the building. The illumination came from back there, a powerful Rochester lamp hanging above a large round table. The light clearly defined the faces of the two people seated at the table and the two men standing alongside it. One of the standing men was Bogardus. And it was Sabina he was talking to, punctuating his words with sharp, angry gestures.

She was pale but composed; whatever fear she might be feeling was contained inside her. It did not look as if she had been abused, at least not physically; her face and upper body bore no marks of violence. She kept shaking her head to whatever Bogardus was saying to her. Quincannon could hear the mutter of his voice, pick out a word here and there, but the sense of his browbeating was unclear.

The other two men in the room were strangers, although Quincannon judged that the mean-looking, fox-faced runt standing next to Bogardus was Conrad. Looking at that one, he felt the pain in his ribs and a sharp cut of hatred along with it. The third man, seated opposite Sabina, was cleaning his fingernails with a skinning knife; Sabina's eyes kept flicking to the blade and away. He was bald and bull-necked with half a yard of jaw, and the expression on his face said that he was enjoying himself.

Quincannon had to fight down an impulse to rush in there, throw down on the three men now, while Sabina was still unhurt. It would be a foolish move, perhaps a deadly one. The time for action was after McClew and his posse arrived — and that time couldn't be far off. The stockade gates were his first priority at the moment, if both he and Sabina hoped to get out of the compound alive.

She would be all right until he got back here, he told himself grimly. Bogardus was taking his time; nothing would happen to her in the next ten minutes.

And when he got back here — then what? At the first inkling of trouble, Bogardus was liable to kill her or try to use her as a hostage. Even if he stormed the place, took them by surprise, there was a chance she would be hurt, a chance he might hurt her himself as he had hurt Katherine Bennett, with a stray bullet — a chance he might not be able to take.

How was he going to get her out of there unharmed?

Chapter 19

Quincannon moved to the rear of the building, waited there while the moon made a brief reappearance and then vanished again. From inside the barn nearby, a steady rattling sound gave him further pause; but then he recognized it — a bridled horse nervously tongue-rolling the cricket in its bit. Either one of the men had neglected to remove the tack from his animal or it was being kept ready for a ride later on. The disposal of another body, maybe, Quincannon thought with banked rage. Sabina's, this time.

He ran silently across to the stockade fence. The shadows that bulked along it hid him as he made his way downhill past the second bunkhouse, around to the gates. They were built of slabwood and held shut by a thick wooden bar set between a pair of iron brackets. Also attached to each half was a vertical iron rod around which a heavy chain could be looped and then padlocked. If the chain and padlock had been fastened, he would have been faced with a difficult decision; as it was, whoever had opened the gate to let Helen Truax and her rig out had not bothered to reset the chain, and it hung loose from one of the rods.

The rod was heavy but he had no trouble lifting it free. He set it aside, slid one of the gate halves open, and stepped out to peer down along the wagon road. The night was empty, hushed. McClew and his men still hadn't shown up; if they were out there now it would be close by, so they could keep watch on the gate, and they would already have signaled him.

He slipped back inside, pulled the gate half almost but not quite shut — open just enough to alert McClew. A thought came to him as he was about to start back the way he had come, along the east side of the fence. Instead he went the other way, around the stamp mill and under the framework of the overhead tram. In the tram's shadow he continued uphill until he reached the stonewalled powder magazine he had noticed that afternoon.

The moon was out again, and when he opened the powder house door, enough of its shine penetrated to give him an idea of how the interior was laid out. He moved inside. Working by feel, he found an open box of dynamite sticks, another of Bickford fuses, a third of small copper detonators. He put two of the sticks and some of the fuses and blasting caps into his coat pocket. Then he backed out of the shed, shut the door, and turned toward the stack of timbers in the middle of the yard.

Downhill, not far away, somebody yelled, "Hey! Hey, you son of a bitch!"

Quincannon wheeled around. The dark shape of a man was running toward him, pawing a revolver off his hip — a skinny little runt, Conrad, drawn outside again by a restlessness or on some damned errand. Everything changed in that instant; all of Quincannon's previous intentions died, all his caution and his advantage of surprise came to an end. A rush of fear seized him, not for himself but for Sabina. His senses all sharpened at once, and he was down on one knee without even thinking about it, his own revolver coming up in his hand.

Conrad's first shot slashed the air harmlessly, made a rocketing explosion in the stillness. Instinct kept Quincannon kneeling instead of throwing himself out flat; the blasting caps in his pocket were volatile and any sudden jarring might set them off.

Another bullet whined off rock to his left — and that was all Conrad had coming to him. Quincannon shot him on the run, heard the man yell, saw him pitch sideways and then fall. By then he was up and running himself, at a downhill slant toward the bunkhouse where Sabina was.

There was a crashing noise from inside the building and the light suddenly went out. A man's voice bellowed an obscenity. Quincannon didn't understand at first what had happened, but the momentary confusion didn't slow him down. Men were just starting to come out of the second bunkhouse, more confused than he was, armed but not knowing what to shoot at. Quincannon was too far away in the darkness for them to see who he was; he might have been one of their own.

In the next second the door of the first bunkhouse burst open. A figure came stumbling out — a figure with flaring skirts bunched high in both hands. Sabina.

Surprise and nascent relief put an end to Quincannon's downhill charge. He shouted at her, "Over here, it's Quincannon!" and saw her break stride, then veer his way. If he had had time to think about what he did next, the ghost of Katherine Bennett might have kept him from doing it. But he acted automatically, the result of years of training: he fired past the running figure of Sabina, emptied his Remington at the cluster of men by the bunkhouse, and drove them back inside or to cover outside.

There were two answering shots, both wild. He saw one man, Bogardus, and then another come barreling free of the darkness inside the first bunkhouse; then Sabina was beside him, and he caught hold of her arm and dragged her back to the long row of timbers. They got around past the end of the rick just as a volley of shots started up from below.

Sabina said breathlessly, "My God, John! I thought . . . I thought I was dead even after I got away from Bogardus. Where did you come from?"

"Never mind that now." He was digging fresh cartridges out of his spares case, jamming them into the cylinders of the Remington. "You can shoot, can't you?"

"I can and I damned well will."

He shoved the reloaded weapon into her hand. "Get down low, back at the corner where you can see, and keep them at a distance."

She didn't ask questions, just did as she was told. Quincannon still had the sticks of dynamite, detonators, and Bickford fuses in his coat pocket; he hauled out one of the fat paper candles, thrust a fuse into one of the little copper tubes. Then he crimped its neck with his teeth and inserted the detonator into the hole punched in the side of the dynamite stick.

Sabina fired at something below; there were half a dozen answering shots.

Quincannon found a lucifer in his pocket, scraped it alight with his back to the wind, and lit the fuse. Immediately he stepped out and hurled the stick toward the bunkhouses, ducking back again as one of the counterfeiters pumped a shot at him.

Somebody shouted, "Dynamite! Look out!"

And the stick blew with a thunderous concussion, filling the night with the stench of its powder fumes. Dirt and pieces of rock showered down out of the haze of smoke. As the echoes rolled away, Quincannon heard one man screaming, another cursing in a steady, mindless litany. He took out the second stick, loaded it while the wind blew the smoke away.

The first blast had torn up earth and rock twenty yards from and midway between the two bunkhouses. One of the koniakers was down on all fours near there, crawling around in circles; he was the one who was screaming. The rest of them had all gone to cover. It was a standoff for the moment, while they regrouped, but it wouldn't be long before they thought to fan out through the compound, try to catch Sabina and him in a crossfire.

Quincannon had another match in his hand, waiting. It was a minute or so before he saw movement again below — men starting to come out of hiding, to slip up to the stable or around to the stamp mill, while others opened fire to cover them. He lit the fuse on the second stick, hurled the dynamite without showing himself. This time the explosion was closer to the main bunkhouse, shattering the glass in its windows, throwing at least one of the counterfeiters off his feet. Quincannon was already moving by then, away from the rick, using the fresh confusion as cover for a run to the powder magazine for more dynamite caps.

But he stopped midway, behind one of the ore wagons, because the smoke was clearing and a shout had gone up, followed by a fusillade of shots. Neither he nor Sabina were the targets now, however; the attention of the koniakers had been focused elsewhere.

McClew and his posse had finally arrived.

Crouched low, running back to rejoin Sabina, Quincannon saw the townsmen come boiling through the stockade gates — a dozen or more, spreading left and right, returning the counterfeiters' fire. The lower section of the compound was like a battleground: men rushing this way and that, men falling, muzzle flashes, powder-smoke, the crack of two-score handguns, mingled shouts and curses and cries from the wounded.

Quincannon took his Remington from Sabina, stood watching tensely. She straightened and clutched his arm. "What is it, John? What's happening?"

"McClew," he said. "He should have had his deputies here sooner, but I'm glad now they were late."

The battle raged for another few minutes. Quincannon could have gone down and joined it, but there was no sense in that. It would have meant leaving Sabina alone.

He said against her ear, "How did you get away from Bogardus and the other one?"

"The shooting distracted them," she said, "and they turned their backs on me. I broke the lantern with my arm and managed to knock Bogardus off his feet on my way to the door. Was it you who started the shooting?"

"No, but I shot the one who did — the little mean-faced runt, Conrad."

"How did you know I was here at the mine?"

"I knew because it's my fault you were abducted."

"Your fault?"

"I'll explain later," he said.

Two of the counterfeiters had broken free of the fighting and were on the run toward the powder magazine. He fired at them, drove them back downhill. The possemen shot one; the other threw his weapon away and surrendered.

Not long after that the gunfire grew sporadic, finally stopped altogether. Quincannon spied McClew running back and forth like a military officer, barking orders that included the mounting of a search for Quincannon and Sabina. That made it time for them to show themselves. Quincannon holstered his revolver and stepped out to hail the marshal, let him know that they were both safe.

Half a minute later they had joined McClew near the main bunkhouse. The marshal wore an exhilarated, satisfied look; his mustaches fairly bristled. "Whoo-ee," he said, "that was some skirmish. Nothing like it around here since the war with the Bannacks in Seventy-eight. You the one exploded that dynamite, Mr. Quincannon?"

"Yes."

"Heard the first blast just as we was setting up outside. We come busting in right away. Would've been here five minutes sooner but we run into Mrs. Truax on the way out from town. Put her in custody and had one of the boys take her back to the jail."

"Good work all around, Marshal."

"Two of you look none the worse for all the fireworks," McClew said. "You are all right, ma'am?"

Sabina nodded. "Yes, thank you."

"Any casualties among your men?" Quincannon asked.

"Couple of flesh wounds is all," McClew said. "T'other side didn't fare half so well. Three dead, four others with holes ventilating their hides."

Quincannon looked over at what was left of the koniakers, grouped together under the guard of half a dozen men and weapons. "Where's Bogardus?"

McClew jerked a thumb at the bunkhouse. "In there. Reckon one of those sticks of dynamite done for him."

The door to the bunkhouse had been blown off its hinges. Someone had found a Betty lamp, lighted it, and set it on top of the Milligan press; as he reached the door, Quincannon could see Bogardus lying sprawled alongside the press, his arms out-flung and his face twisted into a death rictus. The concussion had burst a couple of tins of ink, so that Bogardus had been splattered with the fluid as he was thrown against the press. Along with the blood from his mortal wounds, it glistened blackly in the pale glow from the lamp.

Fitting, Quincannon thought. Bogardus' life had ended as he had sought to live it — with the mixing of spilled blood and printer's ink.

Chapter 20

For the next two days, the main topics of conversation in Silver City were the fight at the Rattling Jack, the unmasking of Bogardus and his crew as koniakers, the arrest of Helen Truax as an accomplice and co-conspirator, and the twin revelations that Quincannon was a Secret Service operative and Sabina Carpenter a Pinkerton detective. The excitement was such that a kind of carnival atmosphere prevailed. Quincannon, Sabina, and Marshal McClew were accorded the mantle of heroes and greeted effusively wherever they went.

Quincannon, however, had little time for socializing. He was kept busy sending wires, questioning prisoners and making arrangements for their transportation to Boise, and coordinating the activities of the other federal officers — among them Samuel Greenspan — who had arrived in Silver. Boggs, who had been both pleased at Quincannon's success and disgruntled that he hadn't waited for official sanction before raiding the Rattling Jack, issued telegraphic orders that all the counterfeiting equipment found at the mine be photographed and itemized in detail for Secret Service files. The Milligan printing press also had to be dismantled, and it and the rest of the equipment shipped to Boise for transshipment east to Washington.

The details of the coney operation that Quincannon did not already know or suspect were for the most part supplied by Helen Truax; she was more than willing to cooperate in order to save her own neck. She also filled in the missing pieces concerning Jason Elder and Whistling Dixon.

The boodle game had been Bogardus' brainchild, in league with Elder, Conrad, and one other man, James Darby, who was now in custody. When the last silver-bearing vein at the Rattling Jack began to peter out, Bogardus and Darby had schemed up the bogus coin idea; Darby had worked as a diemaker and was responsible for the counterfeit eagle and half-eagle molds. Bogardus, meanwhile, had made arrangements through old criminal contacts in Portland and Seattle for the passage of the finished coins.

Bogardus had also, by this time, rekindled his affair with Helen Truax, who had turned up in Silver City as the wife of Oliver Truax. She was bored with Truax, if not with his money, and more than willing to take up with her former lover. She claimed that she hadn't known of his counterfeiting activities until just recently, but Quincannon suspected Bogardus had confided in her almost at once.

The success of his coney coin venture had stirred Bogardus' greed and made him determined to branch out into greenbacks. For that he needed an expert printer and engraver, but not one known to the authorities as a counterfeiter — and the word in Silver was that Jason Elder was such a man. The corruption of Elder had not been difficult; the promise of large sums of money and an unlimited supply of opium had been the bait that landed him. As it turned out, Elder had had the hand of a master and his ten- and twenty-dollar plates were among the best of counterfeits.

While Elder was designing the plates, Bogardus' contacts in Portland and Seattle rounded up the necessary equipment and supplies, mainly through eastern channels, and had them freighted in to Silver City. Their first press had been one of the old single-plate, hand-roller types, but Elder's plates were so good that the press itself didn't matter except in terms of speed of production. The first batch of currency shipped to Portland had excited the gang members there and led to an increasing demand for more queer, which in turn led to the importation of the Milligan press. By this time the Rattling Jack was a factory, with its full attention devoted to the manufacture of bogus notes; the silver-coining end of the game had been abandoned some three months before.

The increased production schedule meant that more men were needed at the mine, and recruits were carefully solicited. One of those recruits, brought in by Conrad, was Whistling Dixon. But he had been a poor choice. Conscience had got the better of him; he had tried once to leave Bogardus' employ, only to be persuaded otherwise by the promise of wealth and by thinly veiled threats. Word of Dixon's skittishness leaked out through the network of boodle carriers and coney dealers and finally reached the ears of the informant Bonniwell in San Francisco.

But the red-haired man, Griswold, had been in San Francisco to meet with the local coney dealer and had gotten wind that Bonniwell was asking questions. He'd gone to Bonniwell's rooming house that night, and murder had been the end result of his visit. His only mistake had been overlooking the piece of paper clenched in Bonniwell's hand, the paper with Whistling Dixon's name on it that had led Quincannon to Silver City.

Meanwhile, in Silver, Jason Elder had also begun to give Bogardus problems. He not only neglected his cover job with Will Coffin's newspaper, but also neglected his work on the production of queer; more and more of his time was spent adrift in the dreamworld wrought by the opium poppy. Bogardus threatened him as a result, and the threat worked only too well: frightened, Elder stole the plates as a measure of self-protection and gave them to Yum Wing.

This shut down the production of counterfeit, of course, and sent Bogardus into a panic. At first he tried to buy back Elder's confidence and thus the plates; Elder was given cash, and when there wasn't enough of that on hand to satisfy him, Bogardus induced Helen Truax to sign over her stock in the Paymaster Mining Corporation. Still Elder balked at returning the plates, thereby signing his own death warrant. Bogardus lost patience and had Elder beaten, then tortured — rough handling that had gone too far, for the printer had died "of a seizure" before revealing the whereabouts of the missing plates.

Desperate then, Bogardus had ordered searches of Elder's shack, the newspaper office, and Will Coffin's house. The second search of the *Volunteer*'s premises had been a reckless and just as futile measure.

With the location of the plates still unknown, the redhead, Griswold, had returned to Silver City with news of what had taken place in San Francisco. The fact that Whistling Dixon was a potential threat to the operation had spurred Bogardus — a murderer already — to order the death of Dixon. Griswold had carried out the order, having accompanied the old cowboy to Slaughterhouse Gulch on a ruse; but he had neglected to search the body afterward, or he would have found the watch Dixon had earlier appropriated from the corpse of Jason Elder.

Then Sabina had found the stock certificate in Elder's shack, and Quincannon had drunkenly given away that fact to Helen Truax. Neither Bogardus nor Mrs. Truax cared that her husband might find out she had signed over her stock; what they were afraid of was any sort of incriminating link between her and Elder. And they were also highly suspicious of Sabina's motives. Mrs. Truax was unaware of her husband's pyramid swindle; it never occurred to her that Sabina's interest might be in him, not her.

It was not until Bogardus read Coffin's second editorial excoriating the Chinese in general and Yum Wing in particular that he realized where the plates must be. Their eventual recovery by Conrad and Darby and the resumption of production at the mine had not completely relieved him, however. He remained suspicious of Sabina, and with his planned departure from Silver City coming imminent, he sought to eliminate all possible threats. He had killed twice; murder no longer bothered him, not even that of a woman.

And now it was finished. Bogardus was dead; Darby and Helen Truax were in jail. So was Griswold, who had been captured on the outskirts of Boise and his wagonload of queer confiscated. Quincannon had been given the names of gang members in Portland, Seattle, and San Francisco — one of the names that of the man who had murdered the boodle carrier in Seattle and dumped his body in Puget Sound — and had telegraphed those names to Boggs. The men were now being systematically rounded up. Boggs' estimation was that the final arrest total would exceed two dozen.

Sabina, too, had been busy. News of his wife's arrest had reached Oliver Truax before dawn on Friday morning and he had fled immediately for fear that his swindling activities would come to light. Armed with this fact, Sabina had persuaded her Pinkerton chief and their clients to press immediate charges of fraud against the mine owner. Truax, who had expected to have plenty of time to clean out his various bank accounts and then find sanctuary, had been arrested in Nampa late Friday afternoon.

Quincannon and Sabina did find time, on Saturday evening, to have a quiet supper at McClew's home. They talked of their work, and tentatively of personal matters; but he did not mention Katherine Bennett's name. He would have liked to tell Sabina about that day in Virginia City, and perhaps someday he would have the opportunity. But not now, not yet.

She observed once that he seemed not to be drinking. He said, "I've been too busy to think about whiskey."

"Then perhaps you don't need it so badly after all, John."

"Perhaps not," he said. "No, perhaps not."

Changes had been wrought inside him; he was not the same man who had arrived in Idaho one week ago. He felt as if he were just emerging from an abyss, one that blind, senseless guilt had dropped him into. He had begun to see things differently now that he was coming out of that abyss. One life had been destroyed, yes, through tragic accident. His guilt and his dependence on alcohol had almost allowed a second — Sabina's — to perish. If he allowed those factors to continue governing him, they *would* destroy a third life — his own this time. What was the sense in that? There were things to be done with his special skills, good things over many years of public service. And weren't those things a proper memorial to the short and tragic life of Katherine Bennett?

On Saturday morning he and Sabina left on the stage for Boise; she had only been leasing the millinery shop and all that went with it, so the closing of it had presented no problem. There was fanfare at their departure — a brass band, the mayor offering an eloquently worded speech — but neither of them paid much attention. Nor did they pay much attention to their fellow passengers on the long ride out of the Owyhees across the plains.

They said goodbye at the new rail depot in Boise. "Will we see each other again, John?" she asked.

"Would you like it if we did?"

"I would. And you?"

"Yes. I've worked in Denver many times; I'll be sent there again soon, I'm sure."

"And I to San Francisco."

"It won't be long, then," he said. But he was thinking that in truth it had been two years since his last visit to Colorado; and that Sabina was an attractive woman with too much to offer to remain an unattached widow for long. There was a sadness in him as he watched her board an eastbound Central Pacific car — a sadness born of something he suspected was much more profound than simple kinship.

Two weeks after his return to San Francisco, following a great deal of deliberation, Quincannon sent a wire to Sabina care of the Pinkerton Agency, Denver. It read:

I AM CONSIDERING RESIGNATION FROM SERVICE TO ESTABLISH PRI-

VATE PRACTICE STOP WOULD YOU
BE INTERESTED IN MOVE TO SF TO
JOIN ME THIS VENTURE QMK
BUSINESS ONLY OF COURSE

He waited anxiously, but not long, for
her reply. It came the next afternoon.

YOUR OFFER A PLEASANT SURPRISE
STOP YES I WOULD CONSIDER IF
EQUAL PARTNERSHIP WHAT YOU
HAVE IN MIND STOP BUSINESS ONLY
OF COURSE STOP IF YOUR ANSWER
AFFIRMATIVE I WILL REQUEST LEAVE
OF ABSENCE TO COME YOUR CITY
FOR PERSONAL DISCUSSION

Quincannon wired his affirmative. Then
he went to the Palace Hotel, and because
he had not had a drink of alcohol in nine-
teen days, he did his celebrating with a pot
of black coffee and a fifty-cent cigar.